Cherished By The Texan

Copyright

First Edition, February 2023
Copyright © 2023 by Melony Ann

Paperback ISBN: 978-1-961966-18-5

Published by: Carxander Publishing
Minnesota

Disclaimer

The books in this series are based completely on dreams that I've had or that one of the other people in my relationship has had. They all have a little bit of real life thrown in so that you, the reader, can get to know us a little bit better.

These books can and should be read as standalone books. There isn't an order to them. All of the characters in the books are the same, as they are all based on characters from real life.

As you read these books, please keep in mind that other than the characters and the city they are based in, these books are not connected to other books in the series. They aren't a continuation of other books. They are all novellas based on dreams that revolve around the same characters.

As you keep that in mind, please enjoy reading this book. I do hope you will also read the others in this series and love them as much as I loved writing them!

Opening Quote

Through the dark, there's a way. There's a love, there's a place, where we don't have to hide. We can dream all night. So, follow me through the sky, and watch the oceans collide. Just keep holding my hand as we're taking off. I know where we'll land. We can escape to a higher plane, in Nirvana state, where the dreamers lay. I'll lay you down, lay you down.

Nirvana by Adam Lambert

Chapter One

☆ DJ ☆

I rub my sweaty palms on my slacks as I watch the judge read from a note one of the guards slipped to her. I bring my hands back up to the table and clasp them together. Judge Lorelei Carpelli lets out a breath and nods slowly. She puts the slip of paper down and looks up.

"Council, approach, please," she commands.

I furrow my brows as I watch. My attorney, Mr. Anderson, pats my arm as he gets up and approaches the bench. I don't move an inch. I keep my eyes forward, my hands folded on the table in front of me. My back is straight. My shoulders are back slightly. I'm trying to portray a confidence I don't fucking feel.

I'm six feet three. I've got the body of a wide-receiver. It's the position I played in high school in a small town in Texas. One I couldn't wait to get the hell out of. I enlisted in the Army and never looked back. I grew up. Got more naturally toned muscles. I became a cop just over twenty-five years ago. It's hard to believe I'm fifty.

I don't really look it. My hair is still dark. Some of it is getting slightly lighter. I have a little bit of gray in my facial hair. But I'm still just as tall, dominating, and intimidating as I was twenty years ago. My workout routine has changed, but I still lift my weights. I still swim my laps. I still do my pull-ups, push-ups, and sit-ups.

Out of the corner of my eye, I see the woman I used to love, the mother of my fourteen-year-old son, smirking. When I married her thirteen years ago, I thought she was everything I ever wanted. Looks? She has them in spades to this day. Blond. Blue-eyed. Perky tits and ass. She's quite a bit younger than me, but the years have been just as kind to her as they have been me.

The problem is, the sweet girl she used to be has morphed into this vindictive, lying bitch who can't keep her legs closed. Well, she can't keep them closed to anyone who glances her way.

Everyone but me.

Which is fine. I haven't wanted to touch her ever since I found out she had a consensual gangbang with a deputy I used to consider a friend and a few of his buddies from his unit. I got an attorney and moved out the very next day, taking my son, Layne, with me.

Didn't take long for my department, the Gainesville, Florida, Police Department, to find out what she did. Mainly because one of the people involved in that gangbang was someone who works under me. He was bragging about banging his Captain's wife.

Captain DJ Rens, GPD's second biggest asshole, second only to my best friend, Lieutenant Matt Chance, lost his wife to a lowly street cop. His words. Not mine. He was promptly fired. His admission proved that he was fucking my wife while he was supposed to be working.

Yeah.

He went over to this gangbang in a department marked squad car with his uniform on while he should have been fucking taking calls.

That was over a year ago. I've been fighting her with the divorce and custody of our son for longer than I thought I would. I thought she'd accept my quite substantial and overly fair monetary settlement and be gone.

I was very wrong. She not only didn't accept. She countered with an outrageous number and asked for full custody of Layne, citing me as both unfit and abusive. Neither of which I am or ever have been. So far, she's brought up my past. My dad beat up my mom. She's attempting to prove it's a cycle that can't be broken. Then, she's given lie after lie about me attacking her and Layne on numerous occasions.

It seems like every single time this entire bullshit shitshow is going to end, she comes up with something else to not only extend my misery, but also to pull Layne into it. His testimony, though it's supposed to help her, always ends up in my favor because, unlike her, he tells the truth under oath. But it pulls him out of school for a day, which pisses me the fuck off even more than I already am that this is still going on.

The judge sighs and nods, visibly as annoyed as I am. Our

attorneys come back to our tables and sit. I notice hers leans over and whispers something to her. The smirk falls from her lips. It causes me to raise an eyebrow, and even though I'm hunched a little as I lean on the table, I glance at my own attorney. He does nothing but wink.

Huh. Interesting.

"I know y'all expected this to end today, but in light of new evidence, we will resume..." She trails off and looks down at her desk. "Well, we'll resume when I can get you on my docket. Court is adjourned." The judge hits her gavel against her desk and stands as the bailiff tells us to rise.

We do, and as she leaves, I turn to Mr. Anderson. "What the hell is going on?" I say only loud enough for him to hear.

He turns to me with a grin. "Looks like the tables have turned on her. The note stated that someone witnessed something this morning as your son was leaving for school. GPD has some evidence they'd like to present. I'll pick it up right now and bring it to the judge. We have a meeting with her in an hour in her chambers. It's why she adjourned us early."

I let out a breath and pinch the bridge of my nose as I look at my watch. It's almost three in the afternoon. "Do you think it's something significant?"

"It's definitely something that will help your case," he says quietly as he gathers his paperwork. My wife, fuck, soon to be ex, I hope, is walking up the aisle sniffling with her lawyer at her side. My lawyer watches her before turning back to me. "You're not going to like this, but there was a report this morning filed against her. Someone saw her hit your son."

It's not possible for the ice in my veins to get any colder. But fuck if it doesn't do just that. I feel like I could burn down the world right after I tear her the hell apart. Limb by fucking limb. I'm even more pissed off that I've been in court all goddamn day and unable to look at my email or my text messages. When I take out my phone, turn it on, and see three voicemails and twelve text messages from Matt, I damn near lose all the control I have.

"Fuck...," I growl under my breath as I start going through them. "She fucking hit him, and he's been out of school all day because he was upset. And didn't want to tell me because of me being in court. Jesus."

Mr. Anderdson pats my arm again. "I'll take care of it. You go be with your son."

I nod as I finish scrolling through messages. When I leave the courtroom, Matt is leaning against the wall with his arms folded over his chest. As soon as he sees me, he drops his arms and falls into step beside me.

"Christ," I let out a breath. "What the hell happened?"

Matt just shakes his head as he walks out to the parking garage with me. I've known him long enough to know that he doesn't want to talk about it here. I don't blame him. My fucking wife probably has spies all over the place. Lord only knows how many of the people in this city she's slept with over the course of our relationship.

Matt walks me to his black Ford F150 truck. "Did you drive here?" he asks as we jump in.

"Yeah. My car's two floors down."

Matt nods and starts the truck. He slowly drives down the ramp. "Layne is with Mariah at her apartment right now. He's okay. You don't need to worry about him. Desiree, though, is getting arrested as we speak."

I feel a lot better knowing Layne is with Mariah. Mariah Carter is one of my best friends. She's the only woman in my life I can count on. Other than those I work with, who I know would have my back if I needed them. At least in the field. Mariah, though, has my back in and out of the field. She's not a cop, but she does have law enforcement training. Not only do I trust her with my life, but she's also the sweetest, most loving, and honest person I know. She'd give me the shirt off her back if I asked for it. Not that it would fit me. The girl is tiny.

As for Desiree, my bitch wife, if I was the kind of man who had no conscience and wouldn't have an issue murdering someone, I would do it in a heartbeat because she deserves it. I'm not that type of man. Though, I am pissed off enough right now. That may just change.

I chuckle, but I'm seething. I shake my head. "Fucking hit him." I look at Matt. "What happened?"

"Well, you know Lyric?"

I raise an eyebrow. "Your fiancé's sister who refuses to come out of her room when you have people over? I can honestly say, nope. Never met her."

He chuckles. "She's very shy. She's also a natural submissive. And she has high anxiety. It makes her anxious to be around too many people. She struggles with people she doesn't know. It took her two days just to look at me and three months to say a word to me." He grins. "I'm exaggerating. But she is shy. She really doesn't like being around people. She'd rather read and work on her graphic designing."

I smile. "How's she doing with that anyway? You said she had a lucrative contract for book covers."

He nods. "She does. And she got it." He looks at me. "I just haven't told her the author she's working for lives in this city less than a mile from where she does." His smile grows wider.

I laugh. "No shit. Mariah? As in my Mariah?"

"Your Mariah?" He raises an eyebrow at me with a smirk. He chuckles and continues before I can retort. "Anyway. Yep. Mariah. She's been talking to her online. She's done designs for indie authors, but never something this big. Mariah is doing a relaunch of her books. She wants new covers and the whole works. Graphics. Everything. It's Lyric's first real job involving graphics. So, she's excited beyond belief for it. Especially when she found out how much she's getting paid. She can't believe it."

"If it works out with her, there's no telling how far Lyric can take it. Mariah is a bestseller with her own publishing company. I knew Rih was working on a deal with a designer, but I didn't put two and two together that her Lyric was the same Lyric who likes avoiding guests."

He chuckles. "I explained to Lyric about just how big and popular Mariah is. How many doors she can open for her. She had a panic attack. Then flew into action. She's been working ever since. It was actually on one of the breaks we forced her to take that she saw it."

"Saw what?"

"Desiree hitting Layne. Lyric was taking a walk after breakfast. She was on her way back when she saw him coming out of the house. Desiree was following him. She was shouting at him as he tried to walk away. She grabbed him. Told him he was a disrespectful asshole like his father, among other things that Lyric really didn't want to repeat, and to not walk away from her when she was talking to him. That he's acting like his good-for-nothing sperm donor. Normally, Lyric hates any kind of confrontation. She fears it. She usually would have run in this situation, but the moment she saw her raise her hand to Layne, she didn't hesitate."

I let out a breath and realize he stopped in front of my car. "Fucking hell. And Layne probably just stood there and took it because he'd never hit a woman. Especially his mother. No matter how much bigger than her he is."

"She stepped in. She has met Layne before when he was hanging out with Beckett. She took Layne home. Desiree tried to fight her, but Layne protected her. Lyric got slapped and had her hair pulled. She has a nasty scratch down the side of her cheek, but she's not seriously hurt. She managed to shove Desiree away hard enough for her to stumble. She didn't want her to accuse Layne of hurting her. She took advantage of her shock when she hit the ground to lead Layne away from the house. By the time I got back home after Lyric called me, Desiree was gone. I knew you'd be in court today, though. I got both of their statements. Got my arrest warrant. I took Layne to Mariah's because Luca was already at work, and Lyric was really upset. She was in tears after I got back. She felt that she should have been quicker. That she could have stopped her from hitting him."

I shake my head, feeling protective of the feelings of the girl I've never met. "She doesn't need to feel like that. You and I know how quickly shit can change. It's often instant. I don't think she even realized right away how far it would go. Desiree, as far as I know, has never hit Layne. Me, yes. But never Layne."

"I actually need to look into that. Lyric told me that it's not the first time she has heard shouting from that house when she was on her walks. She also saw her hit him through the window once. She reported it right away. She knows patrol went to the house because the cop had taken her statement first. But she never heard anything back from it. It has me wondering if we have a cop covering for that bitch. Because after that report, you should have been notified. Child Protective Services should have been called."

I growl low. "He never told me. I was never notified. Didn't see a report. No CPS person ever talked to me. But it pisses me off even more because Layne is with me most of the time. If he'd gotten hit by her even once, he knows I would have had her custody rights revoked completely."

"She never mentioned it to me because she figured I knew and would have seen the report. Anyway, Lyric might be upset with herself because Layne got hurt, but she's more pissed at the neighbors. A few were watching the argument this morning and not intervening. Like it was a fucking soap opera. She actually asked me how many times they stood back and let her hurt him when they heard shouting. If she could hear it from down the street, then they sure as fuck should have."

"She's right." I'm liking this girl more and more.

"That girl might be a natural submissive, but she has a fire inside her that, once lit, is fierce and true." Matt chuckles. "And sass to match it when she wants to. You don't see it at first, but once she's comfortable with you, you get to see her pure personality shine through."

I chuckle but say nothing. Matt knows exactly how to make me like a woman. It's not the first time he's tried to set me up with Lyric over the past year. But he also knows I'm not to that point yet. Leave it to Matt fucking Chance to get me thinking about a woman, though. Asshole.

I smile a little as I rub my forehead. "So, she's been arrested."

"Damn right."

"I can't fucking believe she's done this."

"Well, she's a fucking unhinged little bitch right now. No telling what she'll do." Matt shakes his head. "But I'll tell you what I told Lyric. As much as we hate that it happened, it actually helps Layne in the long run. They have the proof they need to show she's unfit. And from what I overheard him tell Lyric, she'll never get near him again."

I sigh, knowing I need to talk to my son. "It can only go in my favor, right? She should never be able to see Layne again. Let alone have any kind of parental rights over him."

"You never know what the hell kind of story she'll weave out of this. We all know what she said when Layne took her keys so she couldn't drive after that dinner party she threw that left her tipsy."

I close my eyes and shake my head. "Yeah. She said I wasn't allowing her to leave to get to safety after I beat her. I wasn't even fucking there. Thank fuck for Mariah on that one for being my alibi." I open my eyes with a yawn. "I need to get home. I have to talk to Layne."

"Yeah. Wise idea."

I open the door and jump down. "Thanks. For everything. Tell Lyric I said thank you, as well. I know it's gonna be hard, but she might end up getting called in to testify in both the criminal shit and my hearing," I warn.

Matt nods. "I already told her. She doesn't like it. She asked if she could do it through writing or on the phone or something, but she did agree to do whatever it takes."

I nod as I close the door. I get into my car and take a few deep breaths before I'm composed enough to trust myself behind the wheel. I have to talk to Layne. I have to figure out why he didn't tell me what the hell was going on.

I need Mariah.

I need my girl to pull me out of the dark abyss of anger I'm slowly falling into.

Friend.

My friend.

She's my friend.

I need my friend to get me through this bullshit.

"And then he tells me that he's doing this to protect me." I open my eyes and look into Mariah's pretty blue ones. "How the fuck does my own son decide I'm the one who needs protection? He's fourteen!"

Mariah smiles as she runs her fingers soothingly through my hair while she rubs my scalp. I don't remember when she figured out this soothes me, but I'm forever grateful for it. One of my favorite things in the world is lying on her couch, or mine, with my head in her lap, just like I am now, while she listens to me vent about my day. Or vice versa. I love when she's laying in my lap venting about hers while I run my fingers through her hair and listen just as much.

"Well, from what he told me, it has to do with the fact that he thought it could ruin the divorce for you. He didn't want to hinder the chance of you getting custody of him. He knows she twists things. And he knows how much they've hurt you during this process with your divorce. Her lies are what allowed her to have partial custody in the first place. Layne didn't want that. He just wants it to end. And he knew that it was supposed to today."

I sigh and close my eyes again. "I love my son, Rih. But keeping shit like this from me?"

"He thought it was for the best, DJ. He said he didn't even want Lyric to say anything at all. He said it would just cause problems and give her more to argue about to drag this on. He hates what this is doing to you."

"You know, I don't even understand what the hell is happening? I offered her the house. Fuck, I even moved out of it. I took my clothes and car. Very few of the rest of my belongings. I gave her the furniture. Everything in that house. I still pay the damn property taxes on it."

"I know, babe."

"I offered her a fair settlement. Way more than I should have, considering she cheated, and I have the evidence to prove it. I didn't wanna drag Layne through this. I just want her out of my goddamn life. I even offered her joint custody. Even though I know for a damn fact she never wanted Layne."

"I know," Mariah says soothingly.

"And then when she didn't take it and fucking told me she didn't want Layne, I said okay. I gave her a second offer that included more money. I paid off her fucking car." I scowl. "She has a house. A car. Everything in the damn house. A fair monetary settlement. And I told her I'd still pay the property taxes. Still. She said no. And now, she's fighting me for custody of a kid that she doesn't want. Why?"

"Because it means more money, DJ. We've talked about this. It means child support. She gets a huge settlement and child support. It's a lot of extra money each month when you think of it. She'd still be able to live off of you without you being there. She gets everything. The house. The car. The kid. A lot of money. And you know she'd be laughing the whole time because you'd be working your ass off paying the property tax on her house. And paying for her to do nothing at all. You know Layne wouldn't see any of that money, so you'd still be supporting him and paying all of his sports fees and everything else all through college."

I let out a low, dangerous growl because I know she's right. "I just want this bullshit to end."

"I know, DJ. And it will. But I think we're in for a fight. Like more than what we already have been."

I smile a little at that and open my eyes again. "We?"

She laughs and looks down at me. Her beautiful, long brown hair falls over her shoulder as she smiles that megawatt smile she reserves just for me. My heart melts a little. Feelings stir in my gut that I push down and ignore. Mariah is a friend. Nothing more. It's all she'll ever be. I can't let myself feel anything other than that.

Even if she is the only one who has ever managed to make those mystical butterflies take flight. Well... her and a woman I've never fucking met.

"Of course, we. Do you think I'm going to allow you to do this on your own? Come on. Who would I be if I let that happen? I've been in this with you since the beginning."

Of course she's right again. My friendship with her is one of the things Desiree has brought up in court. She's tried to make it that I was cheating on her. I've never done that. I never would. But it's how she retaliated against me for all of the misdeeds that I called her out on. The gangbang was really just the start. Afterwards, I'd found out about several more, mostly from those I work with who felt bad. While I appreciate the honesty and the willingness to talk to the judge on my behalf, I'll still never trust them as far as I can throw them.

I sigh deeply as I sit up. I lean my head back against the couch. "Fuck, this needs to end. It's affecting my job. My son. A woman I've never met. You." I shake my head. "Who knew she'd take it this far?"

"Ooh!" Mariah raises her hand. "Pick me! Pick me!"

I laugh just before I start tickling her. She squeals and giggles as she squirms against me. "You knew, huh?" I keep tickling her.

"Ah! DJ! Stop!" She laughs as she tries to shove me away. Then laughs harder when I hit the spot on her ribcage that makes her almost always give in to whatever I want. She wheels backwards until she's on the couch on her back, just out of my reach.

But not for long.

I shift and straddle her, tickling her again. She laughs harder and arches as she wiggles. She bucks up into me, hitting my dick and instantly making me hard.

Fuck.

I grip her wrists as she squirms, trying to get away, and pin them above her head. I lean down, more to hide my growing problem than anything else. Her coconut shampoo hits me first. Then the coconut, coffee, and vanilla scent of her skin.

Double fuck.

Her smile and laughing eyes do nothing to help. I should run before she sees what she's done, but I don't. I give in and lean in further, mesmerized by her eyes. When she realizes what's about to happen, her eyes widen in shock, but her lips part slightly.

"DJ...," she whispers just before she closes her eyes.

I let my lips claim hers. Mine. She's always been mine. My heart skips a beat just before it seemingly blows up in my chest and relocates to my throat. I've imagined my lips on hers many times over the course of our friendship, but nothing beats the reality. Mariah's mouth is soft. She submits to me, opening her mouth just enough for me to slide my tongue inside.

"Christ...," I murmur. She tastes even better than I dreamed. Her lips are like a mocha latte. My fucking favorite. It must be her lip gloss.

Her tongue meets mine and fireworks seem to explode. Everything fades but her. My need for her. My want. My insatiable desire. The part that knows if I keep this up, I'm never going to be able to fucking stop.

Yet, I don't pull away. I ignore that little voice, and I keep going. I push myself down and grind my dick into her pussy. She moves against me. I catch her sexy whimpers and moans as I kiss her like I'm a starving man and she's my last meal. I let go of her wrists and wrap one arm around her, deepening the kiss. I grab her supple ass and pull her into me so she can feel me.

Why the fuck am I letting this go on?

My dick strains against my jeans, begging me to release it, but I can't let go of her long enough to. Not with the way she's bucking into me. The way her hands are digging into my shoulders. She tastes even better the longer my tongue fucks her mouth, much the way my cock wants to. The way I want to.

Holy shit. Why the fuck am I not running?

Because she feels way too good. Because I'm a selfish motherfucker who wants nothing more than to give into the primal urge I have to bury myself in her pussy and never come out. To claim her as mine because she rightfully fucking is.

But I don't get the chance. As my mouth is dominating hers, she starts trembling. Her eyes widen, and she bites my lip as her body stiffens. Her nails dig into my shoulders as she bunches my shirt into her fists.

"Oh fuck," I whisper when I realize what's happening.

"Oh, DJ!" Her head falls back as she bucks into me. Her pussy pushes against my dick again and again as her orgasm takes complete control.

I have no chance to stop mine. I feel a sharp jolt shoot down my spine, and I come harder than I think I've ever come for anyone. "Holy shit, Rih," I moan as I press my cock harder against her. I drop my head and bury my face in her hair. "Fuck."

I don't know how long I lay with her like that, the front of my jeans as soaked as her thin as hell booty shorts, but her sexy whimpers bring me back to reality with such violent force that I jump and abruptly pull away. We're both panting. I scramble to my feet and watch her slowly come out of a daze with a soft smile on her lips. She starts to sit up as her eyes meet mine.

"Rih, I… uh… didn't… I…" I look towards the door. "I… gotta go. I have to make sure Layne is ready for bed."

"O-okay," she stammers.

I feel her eyes on my back as I damn near run for the door. I only live a few apartments down from her. I was lucky her complex had an opening when I needed it. That doesn't happen in Gainesville often. We're a college town and have a bit of a housing crisis.

Before I open the door to my apartment I lean against the wall and take several deep breaths. I'm not going to lie to myself and say I haven't wanted to kiss Mariah. Hell. A lot more than that. I won't even try and tell myself that I haven't gotten myself off to thoughts of her. In my head, the girl is already mine.

But I am not in the state of mind or position to start a relationship with anyone. Especially her. Mariah and I are close friends. We have been for years now. I would never want to do anything to jeopardize that.

Maybe.

What could one night hurt? To get it out of my system. To get it out of hers. I heard her moans and whimpers. I felt her underneath me. I felt her come, clinging to me as she rode out the only orgasm a man has ever given her.

Yeah.

I know that.

I know everything about her. I know the only person who has ever made her come is herself and her trusty pink vibrator.

And now me.

I shake my head. No.

Fuck no.

Absolutely not.

This can't happen. That was a one time thing. No more. Nothing. Not now.

Not ever.

I need to get all crazy ideas I have of her and I together anywhere other than my mind out of it. Immediately. She's not mine in real life. Only in my fantasies. It's the only way it's ever going to be.

Chapter Two

✫ Mariah ✫

What just happened? I run my thumb over my lower lip and blink at the door DJ nearly ran out of. I've never seen him do that before. *Did I say something wrong? Was I not a good kisser? Did my breath smell bad? Did I move awkwardly? Should I not have come? Should I have shoved him off or something? What did I do wrong?*

I shakily stand and slowly make my way to the door. Hands trembling, I lock it, then stare at it in confusion as I wrap my arms around myself. That was the best experience I've ever had. It was the best everything I've ever had. I've only been with two men, not including DJ, but not one of them ever made me come. But I must not have done it right. It must have been terrible for him if he ran off like that.

I take a few steps backwards before I slowly turn around. I sit down on the couch with my arms locked around me and blink a few times. I see nothing but DJ in front of me and feel that rush of pleasure on repeat. But it's him leaving so quickly, like he was trying to dodge a bullet, that keeps circling around my head like a whirlwind.

I had to have done something wrong. Did I bite him? Did I move the wrong way? Did I not show him that I was enjoying it and okay with it happening? We've been friends for a long time. Maybe he's afraid he'll ruin our friendship.

I shake my head and start cleaning up the hot chocolate I made for us when DJ came over. I bring them to the kitchen and start washing the few dishes I have for the day and try not to think about what happened. The logical part of me knows that DJ doesn't want to be in a relationship right now. I know that he's wanting to put everything with his bitch of a soon-to-be-ex-wife behind him. He wants custody of his son and wants the divorce to be finalized.

I also know I'm not the kind of woman he likes. He goes for blond, blue-eyed women who look like a Barbie. I'm not that. I actually have hips, boobs, and an ass. I have curves. A lot of them. It's taken me a very long time to get to the point of liking who I am. People have told me over and over again throughout my life that I'll never be pretty enough or skinny enough or good enough. Those words eventually engraved themselves in my brain.

I sigh as I walk back to my couch and take out my laptop. I was getting really good at seeing myself in a new light. DJ had a huge hand in that. He's been a large part of giving me the confidence I needed to let my past stay there. Without him, I don't think I'd be who I am today. I wouldn't have become a bestseller. I certainly wouldn't own my own publishing company.

Granted, I don't run it. I hired someone who knew what he was doing, but it's still mine. And I never would have been able to do that without DJ's guidance and support. He believed in me when no one else did.

He was the one who picked me up and put me back together when I first moved here. I was a very broken soul. DJ saw a diamond in the rough. He made me feel pretty for the first time in my life. He helped me to realize my dreams. He spent so much time building up my confidence.

I've been secretly in love with him since I first met him. I've never told him because I'm not the type to ruin relationships. No matter how crappy the relationship is. I was happy to be his friend. I am. I am happy to be his friend. He's one of the few I have. Matt, his partner on the force, and Matt's fiancé, Luca, are all I have.

Lyric. I haven't met her, but Lyric Sharpe is quickly becoming one of my favorite people. She's a cover designer who I have enlisted to help me rebrand some of my work. Hell, all of it. And me. She's created a logo and several covers already. I've already created an entire campaign for myself regarding the relaunch of my first series and myself.

I smile a little despite my confusion over DJ and open my chat with Lyric, hoping she's on. She always makes me feel better. She's not online. If I'm being totally honest, it's a good thing. She works such long hours.

I'm also a little in love with her. Hell, probably a lot in love with her. I don't know when it happened, but she's the first woman I've ever truly had feelings for. Even though I've known most of my life that I'm pansexual. So, considering I'm already confused about everything that just transpired with DJ, it's really best that she's not online. Hopefully, she's asleep. She needs it.

Instead, I work on my campaign and allow myself to get lost. It's what good writers do, right? They get lost in their work and pretend the outside world doesn't exist. They pour their heart and soul into the work. Give it their all. It's why I am where I am.

But after not getting anything done, I'm shutting down and pacing my living room. I run my fingers through my hair and scrub my hands down my face as I look at the clock then eye my phone. DJ has insomnia and PTSD from his time in the military. If he sleeps, he doesn't often get there until late into the night or early morning hours. If I call him now, would I wake him?

I shake my head. "You're being stupid, Mariah," I say to myself. "Ridiculous. He kissed you. He made the first move. He wouldn't have done that if he didn't want to. He gave you the best orgasm of your life. He probably freaked himself out or thought I was mad. We're friends. He just had one of the most stressful days in his life. Stop overthinking this."

I nod after giving myself a pep talk and pad directly to my shower. I didn't forget that I'm soaked from coming, though I feel pretty dry now. I had to calm down enough to think straight. My head was spinning in so many different directions.

I love my shower. The shower head has the perfect pressure for any mood. Right now, it needs to be a hard spray because I have to relax and stop thinking. Everyone likes a massage. Even if it is from a shower. Right?

I strip down and turn my playlist on my phone on after adjusting the water temperature and pressure. Before I can think anything of it, I step into the shower and relish in the hard water pressure beating on my back. Just have to keep my eyes open. It'll all be just fine.

"Mmm…," I moan quietly. I lean my elbows and forearms against the shower wall and try to force all thoughts of DJ and writing out of my mind.

I just need to be. Then maybe I can think and figure out what happened with DJ.

But even the water beating down on me and helping release the tension in my body doesn't help to ease my mind. The demon in my head keeps saying over and over that I fucked things up with my best friend. That he'll never want to talk to me again. I'm a horrible kisser. I taste bad. I'm revolting. I shouldn't have lost control and come in my shorts. It's gross. I'm gross. A guy like him will never ever be with someone like me. I'm not his type. I'm disgusting. I'm not pretty enough. I'm too fat. I'm not smart enough. Not good enough.

I cover my ears and squeeze my eyes shut to drown out my demon's voice. I know he isn't right. I know he's lying. Trying to bring me down. He's fucked with me my whole life, but the older I've gotten, the more powerful he's gotten.

And he doesn't shut up.

He continues berating me and keeps telling me I'm awful. That I ruined my relationship with DJ. That he'll never want to see me again.

I'm alone.

My eyes fly open and my head snaps towards the shower door. Why were my eyes closed? I never close my eyes in the shower! Not since…

The music! Where's the music? Why isn't it playing? The hair on the back of my neck stands on end. I shiver. I'm being watched. I can feel it with every fiber of my being.

My head snaps behind me. I see a dark shadow that disappears.

My heart pounds at a beat that is why too fast. I want to scream, but I can't.

Behind you! my demon screams. *He's behind you!*

19

I quickly turn, nearly falling, and look behind me again. There's nothing but a wall. Where's the music? Why isn't the music playing? Why did I close my eyes?

I let out a quiet squeak and quickly turn back to the shower controls. I shut the water off and shiver again. Like I'm being watched.

Behind you!

"Ah!" I squeak out as I turn again.

Nothing. No one.

But I see him. He's there. Tall. Reddish blond hair. Green eyes. Scrawny, but he's taller than me. Way bigger. He towers over me. He reaches for me with a soulless smile and twinkling eyes.

Run! Run!

I listen to my demon for the first time today and reach for the shower door. Though, I'm positive it's not me making the motions. I'm sure I've been possessed and the demon in my head is taking over.

All I can hear is his voice; my heart pounding.

Behind you!

"Ah!" I squeak out again.

My feet hit the linoleum. I slip, but scramble to keep from falling. I grab the towel I left by the door. As soon as my feet hit the carpet in the hallway, the chill gets more intense. I'm being chased. I know it. All I can think of is getting out.

DJ.

He'll help.

He won't. You fucked that up.

I shake my head and try to get air into my lungs. I put my hands over my face and sit down in my oversized chair near the floor to ceiling window in my living room. I try to focus on taking deep breaths. I try to push everything out of my mind.

Him. My attacker. He's not real. He's not here. I'm safe. I'm in my safe place. My safe chair.

Behind you! He's there!

"No! He's not here! He's not!" I scream.

I can't breathe. Tears are streaming down my face. Tears I had no idea I was crying. I rock back and forth, clutching the towel around my body. I try to ignore the demon. I try to fight him. I know he's not behind me. I know it.

But the shivers are intense.

Don't blink! Run!

Once again, the demon wins out. I run. I grab my keys from the table by my door as I unlock it. At least I thought to do that. That has to count for something. I can think. I'm not too far gone.

I feel someone touch my shoulder, and it spurs me to listen to the demon again and run faster. In nothing but a towel, I flee to the only person I know can make it all stop. How could I have been so stupid to think I could deal with a shower? I don't love them at all. I hate everything about them. I can hardly deal with them even with my music.

When I reach DJ's door, I'm fairly convinced I'm going to die. Whether it be from not being able to get air into my lungs or being killed by *him*, though, I'm not sure. I knock on the door, gasping for breath. The demon is screaming at me that he's behind me. That he's going to kill me this time right after he fucks me. My throat is closing up. My vision is getting darker because I'm hyperventilating.

Consciously, I am fully aware of what's happening. I keep rapidly knocking, even though I don't hear it. Is it loud enough? The logical person in me is locked away and can't come out. It's like there's a metal cage in the back of my mind. Like she's watching through my eyes as I spiral and can't do shit to help me. She's trapped. She's rattling the metal bars of the cage, but nothing is budging.

"Mariah?" DJ asks when he opens the door. His Southern accent is thick when he's tired or just waking up. I love his accent. "What's happening?"

I can't say anything. All I can do is look at him; plead with him to give me what I need, though I can't articulate what it is.I don't even know. I just need him to fix it. Fix it like he always does. Make it stop. My lungs burn. My chest hurts. My throat is on fire. My head is starting to feel light.

"D...J...," I finally manage to squeak out over my terror as DJ rubs his eyes.

He looks down at me and yawns. "Honey, it's three in -" He cuts himself off. Three in the morning. I hadn't realized I'd gotten so lost and that much time had passed. His eyes widen when he's finally focused enough to see me. "Jesus Christ, baby." He pulls me into him and picks me up. He kicks the door closed and locks it as I wrap my arms around his shoulders and bury my face in his neck.

His scent.

Him.

He doesn't love you. He doesn't even like you. You fucked up. Why are you even here? Stupid girl.

DJ carries me, holding me close. I squeeze my arms around him as I tremble. "What happened to you, Rih?" he whispers.

"I…" I squeak with every sob. I gasp for air. I can't get enough. I try so hard to focus on him, but I can't. The demon is winning.

"Dad?"

Layne. He's here. I woke him up.

"Go back to bed, buddy. I got her. She'll be okay."

I feel Layne's eyes on me as DJ walks with me somewhere. I'm paying no attention to my surroundings. I can't. I can't move. I'm paralyzed. I can't feel my body anymore. Am I dead? Did the demon succeed in dragging me to hell?

DJ somehow manages to get me onto his bed and wrap around me without letting me go. I think it's his bed. I hope my mind isn't playing tricks on me.

"Breathe, honey." He tangles his fingers in my hair and presses my ear against his chest. "Listen to my heartbeat," he whispers into my ear. "Just me and you. Focus on my breathing." He keeps breathing steadily. Breath after breath. "You're okay. You're safe. I'm here. Right here, honey," he murmurs into my hair. "No one is going to get you. He's not here. It's just me and you."

I don't know how he does it. I don't know how he always knows what's going on in my head without me saying it. Whether it's the demon. Or whether it's *him*. DJ always knows.

Several moments pass. My breathing becomes more and more steady. The demon's voice fades further and further into the darkness where he resides. I feel safer and safer wrapped in him. Breathing him in. His fresh, earthy scent. Unique to him.

DJ.

It's not the only time I've ended up like this with him. The first time I had a panic attack was in a coffee shop. DJ was in the middle of telling me something when a crowd of people came in. I don't remember much after that, but DJ promised me that day that he'd always be here for me. That he'd always help me through it. No matter what time of day or night it was.

And he was. Day or night, DJ was always available to me. He has talked me down from so many panic attacks, I've lost count. For a long time, it was just his deep, soothing, and dominant voice over the phone. Then when he moved just down the hall for me, I spent my panic attacks burrowed in his arms.

In him.

Even when the panic attack wasn't bad, DJ never left me to fight alone.

"I tried to take a shower," I finally whisper, though I have no idea how long it's been.

DJ's arms tighten around me. "I gathered. It's not normal for you to run around in nothing but a towel." I can feel his teasing smile against my neck.

I smile softly. "I made the mistake of closing my eyes. I don't remember doing it. I was just trying to relax." The barely there soft hair on his chest brushes my cheek and grounds me even more.

"And you saw him," DJ whispers.

"Not at first," I whisper. "Robert appeared later. It was the demon at first screaming that he's behind me. When I turned, he wasn't there. No one was. What triggered it all was the music on my phone stopped playing. The demon made me think that someone had stopped it and was in there with me."

"I know, honey. We've talked about this. And I always tell you the same thing. Your demon is a fucking asshole. You're okay. You're safe. He's never going to hurt you again, right?"

I nod and slowly sit up as I sniffle. DJ is the only one who knows my entire life story. The only one who knows what happened to me when I was younger. I've never told anyone else why I can't take showers without panicking. Or why I sleep with a fan on all the time.

It was because Robert attacked me in the shower. He shoved me against the shower wall and jammed his fingers inside me until he came on my back and butt. I was seven. Not long after that, he snuck into my room and held a pillow over my head while he tongued me while he was fingering me. I couldn't breathe. The longer I screamed, the harder the pillow was held. I passed out. When I came to, he was cleaning his come off me.

I blocked out those memories. I had no idea why I freaked out in the shower or got scared if there was no air circulation while I slept. Not until a couple of years ago when those memories slammed into me.

The only person who knows is DJ. He was the one who pulled me out of the darkness I was forcefully dragged into. I wouldn't have survived without him.

DJ sits up and wraps an arm around my waist. He rests his chin on my shoulder. "What else did the demon say?"

I let out a quiet huff. "I'm not sure I want to tell you that."

He hugs me tighter to his side. "Really? We're playing this game? You tell me everything, Rih. I know everything about you. From your favorite foods all the way down to which panties you like to use when you have your period. I know how heavy the flow is by how often you go to the bathroom. I know your mood by the color of your eyes." He squeezes me tighter. "What else did that fucker say to you? I can't combat it if I don't know."

"I don't want to upset you, DJ," I say quietly. "You have enough going on without adding me and all of my insanity to it." I shake my head. "I'll get over it. I'm a forty-year-old woman. I shouldn't have gotten so worked up over what happened anyway."

"Ahh… There it is. The reason behind everything that happened to you tonight. The reason for the spiral."

I bite my lip. Sometimes, I completely forget how smart he is. How easy it is for him to put pieces together and read people without them saying a single word. Or saying very little. "I don't want to talk about it." And I really don't. I know how foolish I'm being. I know he doesn't want me like that. It was a mistake.

"Rih, we can't not talk about that." He cups my cheek and turns my face so I'm looking at him. "I'm sorry. I shouldn't have kissed you like that. I definitely shouldn't have made you come like that. I was upset about what happened today. I wasn't thinking right. My mind wasn't in the right place." He kisses my forehead and gently tugs me down so I'm laying with him.

I let out a breath and close my eyes. "I should go," I whisper.

And I should. I know way too much about how good he feels against me. All of him. I know how hard and big he is. I know what he feels like when he comes. I know the sounds he makes as he chases his orgasm. I know how good he smells when he's coming down after. All things I shouldn't know. All things I should run from and forget.

But most of all, I know how it feels to have my heart break with his words of regret. That he shouldn't have done what he did.

"Not a chance in hell." He hugs me tighter. "Not after that. You're staying right here." The dominance in his voice soothes me almost as much as it saddens me because I need that but will never have it in any other form but this.

Just friends.

I sniffle. "Don't be upset about what happened," I say as bravely as I can. "I…" I can't finish. I want to say I'm not upset, but I can't lie to him. I've never been able to do that. I never will. "Can I get a t-shirt?" It's not the first time I've borrowed one of his t-shirts and slept in his bed. But today feels very different than all of the others.

DJ watches me for a few moments before he sighs and gets up. He hands me a t-shirt as I make my way to his bathroom. I slip the towel off and hang it on his door, then find the brush I left here a long time ago to brush out my nearly dry and very snarled hair. When I finish, I walk back to his bed and crawl under the covers. DJ snuggles me close to him.

"I *am* sorry, Rih. I didn't mean for it to happen," he whispers as his arms tighten around me.

"It's okay," I whisper back. "I'm…" I trail off and let out a breath.

I can't finish the sentence because it's a lie. A vicious one. I am upset, but not upset that it happened.

I'm upset with myself for *wanting* it to.

Chapter Three

✫ Lyric ✫

I take a breath as the car pulls up to the police station in downtown Gainesville. I love Florida. It's always warm. And the people here are really nice. For the most part. Not like I really go out much. I prefer staying home and around my neighborhood. But sometimes, like today, I'm forced out of the sanctuary I call my bedroom. That's not to say that the whole house isn't my sanctuary, but there is something about my bedroom that is like an extra layer of security for me.

I sigh as I close the door to the car and look up at the headquarters building with a pout. *You can do this, Lyric.* I nod resolutely and walk into the building. I've been here before. I know the place is safe.

I stop at the front desk. The older woman who is the receptionist here smiles at me. "Hey, Lyric! I haven't seen you around for a while."

I swallow hard, but I smile. "Just had to drop off something for Matt."

A police officer comes in behind me holding the arm of the literal definition of thug. He's cocky as hell and radiates the scent of the worst scented weed I've ever had the misfortune of smelling.

"Oohwee, Mamacita. Look at you, sexy girl," the thug says in the worst Mexican accent I've ever heard. I wrinkle my nose. He doesn't look like he has any kind of Hispanic heritage whatsoever.

"Shut up," the cop growls. "Unless you want our Lieutenant to lock you up with the Baiters."

"I ain't scared of no bitch fags," the Marcus Consuelos wannabe barks. I growl a little and glare at his back at the derogatory term that fell from his ugly lips.

"Stupid asshole," I say quietly as the cop shoves him through a door. I turn back to the receptionist behind the desk.

"You can go back, Lyric. He just finished up with an interview. He'll be in his office."

"Thank you." I glare at the door the cop took the shitsucker through as I make my way into the office area of the department. I smile when I see Lieutenant Matt Chance standing outside his office door waiting for me.

He looks up and grins. "It's nice seeing you out of the house."

I stick out my tongue. "I hate being out of it."

"Oh, I know." He leans down and pecks the top of my head, then waits for me to step inside his office before he closes the door. "You know I would have survived without lunch. I have a credit card and a truck."

I wrinkle my nose. "Takeout is bad for you. And I know how much you hate having to resort to it." I sit down and place the cooler lunch bag on his desk. "I also know you're a much bigger fan of what's in there than you are of Subway."

He smiles as he sits in the chair behind his desk. "I won't lie and say whatever is in there smells much better than Subway."

I giggle as I lean forward and unzip the bag. "Did everything go okay with that call that had you rushing this morning?"

"Uh. Yeah. For the most part. We caught the guy we were after. He's been good about giving us names and locations of all the other fuckers involved." He leans back in his chair. "I actually thought he was just giving us a bunch of shit. But I sent out some guys to a few of these places and was quite shocked to see them all there. Turns out the fucker's biggest fear is going to prison. So, he was being as cooperative as possible with me, hoping for a deal."

"Isn't this the drug guy?"

Matt nods. "Yep. The one dealing to elementary kids a block away from the school." He rolls his eyes. "Like he's invisible or something. He honestly thought he had a good thing going and wouldn't get caught."

I shake my head and take out the sandwich I made for him. "I hope he gets the book thrown at him. Poor kids."

"Justice will be served." He takes the sandwich I hand him. "Smells incredible. What is it?"

"Chicken and stuffing. But I'm not sure you'll like it. I shredded the leftover chicken from last night and mixed it with the stuffing. It can be a little dry, though, so I added some honey mustard dressing." I reach back into the bag. "I made some fruit bars, so I brought you one of those for dessert. And if you're still hungry, I made a side salad and used the rest of the chicken on top with some feta cheese." I pull out the salad. "And I also put some honey mustard dressing and some ranch dressing in here." I put the dressings on top of the Tupperware bowl with the salad and pull it out of the bag. I hand it to him, then slide the fruit bar across his desk.

"You're spoiling me. Is this your way of trying to steal me away from Luca so you can play out all of your dirty crush fantasies with me?" He gives me a teasing grin as he takes a bite of the sandwich.

I laugh. "Don't you wish."

He grins and winks. "I'm onto you, Sharpe."

I giggle and blush. When I first met Matt, I really did have a bit of a crush on him. I knew he and my brother were together, but Matt is truly hot. He's tall. Like six feet four. He's got sexy coffee colored eyes that match the brown, messy, short hair that sits on his head. He's muscular and is very well-built. He carries a six pack of abs that he isn't afraid to show off, and both of his arms are covered in tattoos. He's every girl's and guy's dream come to life. The dark scruff he has on his face only makes him sexier.

I got over the crush rather quickly, but I did open up to him and admit it after I got to know him and became close with him. He's more like my big brother now. More than a friend, for sure. Much closer than that. He's one of the two people in my life that I really consider family. Once I came out of my shell around him, I was very glad to have him in my life. Each day that passes, that gratefulness grows.

Matt is just as supportive of me as Luca is. He's encouraged my designing dream. He's done so much to help Luca help me with my anxiety and self-confidence issues. He's even done more than I can ever express to help me with my body image issues and my self-worth problems. I've gone through a lot in my life. I'm not sure I would have survived in the United Kingdom much longer, so I'll always be thankful to fate for introducing Matt to Luca. Without Matt, Luca and I would probably not be here in the United States where we belong. It's always been our dream to live here. The United Kingdom just wasn't home to us anymore. I don't think it ever really was.

I shake my head slightly to rid myself of all the thoughts running through my head. When I focus back on Matt, he's watching me and chewing his sandwich. I smile softly. It's my way of letting him know I'm okay.

"Where did you just go right there?"

I shake my head. "Nowhere." I lean back in my chair. "I was just thinking."

"About…?"

"Mostly how I'll always be grateful to whatever hand played a part in getting you and Luca together. And how I don't think I would have thrived in the United Kingdom. I don't think I would have made it all. I was pretty much done with life there." I look down at my hands after admitting that. I hate remembering how low I got. Honestly, I'm not sure how far from the truth that actually is. If I hadn't had Luca… I shake my head again.

Matt nods slowly as he finishes his sandwich. "You know, you've never told me the whole story."

I keep my eyes lowered. "I always assumed Luca had."

Matt chuckles a little and picks up the salad. "It's not his story to tell, sweetheart."

I've lived here for five years now. Luca has been here for six years. When we first decided we were going to move here, Luca did it first because he wanted to have things set up for me when I did. But my twin brother leaving me was something I wasn't as prepared for as I thought I was.

Luca and I are both thirty-one-years old now. We may have been born a few minutes apart on the very same day, Luca coming out before me, but our differences are vast. We really don't look anything alike. Just our eyes. A very pretty hazel with flecks of gold. His brown hair is lighter than mine. He's six feet. I'm just five feet three.

I've always joked that he was a greedy fucker when we were in the womb. He inherited all of the good looks and genes possible. I am exactly the opposite of him in every single way. I have curves. He has muscles for days. I'm very introverted. He can start a conversation with literally anyone and become their best friend. I'm very shy and submissive. He's so outgoing and dominant.

Luca had a very easy time in school. I struggled beyond belief. Not that I couldn't keep up or got bad grades. But I was bullied and pushed around. Luca did all he could to protect me and keep it from happening, but he couldn't be around all of the time. Not to say he didn't try.

Truthfully, Luca was all I had for most of my life. When we decided to move here, it was because of me. He knew even before I did the path I was on. The spiral that was leading me to a very dark abyss. I was very, very depressed. I couldn't get any kind of help because the United Kingdom just doesn't work like that. My doctor wouldn't prescribe me anything to help with my anxiety or depression, and it just got worse and worse. If Luca hadn't realized what was happening with me, I know I'd be dead today.

"If you're not ready, Lyric, I'll never force you," Matt says quietly.

I blink a few times. "I hate when I get lost in thoughts." I take a deep breath. "I'll tell you tonight. I promise. You deserve to know. You're family."

"Just know you're not in this alone. You have me and Luca. And you've been getting along very well with that author you're designing for."

My eyes widen at the thought of Mariah Marie. "Oh my God. I got my first payment installment today." I can feel my cheeks heat and darken to a crimson color as I look up at him. "Do you know how much it is?"

He smiles as he finishes his salad. "How much?"

"She's paying me five hundred dollars per cover. That's more than double what I was charging authors. She has nine books. Well, more than that, but for this part of it it's nine. For the first four? Two thousand dollars, Matt. I don't even know what to do with that kind of money!"

He laughs and puts the empty bowl down. He picks up the bar after taking a long drink of the water in his water bottle. His brown eyes glimmer with secrets. It's not the first time we've talked about Mariah and

I've seen that same look. I narrow my eyes because I know he's hiding something.

"I heard she has her own publishing company. She employs some guy to run it for her. He's a good friend, I guess. His dad runs another publishing company. I guess this guy wanted to stick it to his father. So, he accepted the offer and helped Mariah grow it to beyond her wildest expectations. Even stole some of his dad's authors."

I nod and giggle. "She told me that. His name is Tyler Alexander. And Mariah is a bestseller herself. She was talking about hiring me to work exclusively for her company, but I can't do that to all of my independent authors. So, do you know what she said to that?"

He smiles. "What?"

"She said that was totally fine. That she still wants to hire me to work with her company, but that I can still work independently. It would mean that every single author who they work with would be using my services. Matt, I'd never be out of work!"

He laughs. "That's what you've wanted, right? The ultimate goal?"

I nod enthusiastically with a huge smile. "This is incredible. And it's not just these nine books. She's having me design covers for all of her books. She has so many."

"It sounds to me like this turned out to be a pretty great opportunity for you."

"So good. And she's such a sweet person. I love talking to her. Sometimes, because she has anxiety like I do, she's up in the middle of the night. She talks to me until I fall back to sleep. She's so soothing. Even if it is just on chat. She just has this way about her. I really, really like her." A lot, but I leave that part out.

Matt smiles again. "She's a good girl."

I tilt my head at that but shake it off. I'm sure everything I've said about her would lead him to that conclusion. I talk about her a lot. What I haven't told him or my brother is that the reason I talk so much about her isn't because of the work. It's because she's everything I've ever wanted in a significant other. She's sweet, smart, creative, genuine, and has integrity that spans the globe. She's protective of others and fights for what she believes in, even though she has anxiety, and speaking out is so hard for her. She's even got a bit of a dominant streak to her that sometimes sends chills all throughout me.

"I really do like her."

Matt raises an eyebrow. "Like... you... like her? Or you really, really like her?"

"Like I really, really wanna zig-a-zag-ah." I quip, giggling. I am *not* a fan of the Spice Girls, but I couldn't resist.

Matt laughs. "Well, that's interesting. I never thought I'd see the day little Lily had a genuine crush."

"You are definitely an asshole." I can't help the flush that appears in my cheeks at the childhood nickname that only my brother has ever called me. A name Matt has since taken to calling me, too.

He grins and winks. "I know. It's one of my best qualities."

I laugh. "I don't understand how Luca puts up with you."

"I'm really good in bed."

"Eew. Stop it. I don't want to know."

Matt laughs as he starts gathering up the garbage from his lunch. "Thank you for this. It was delicious. I don't know what I did to deserve it, but let me know so I can keep it up."

I give him a soft smile. "I just wanted to do something nice for you. Mostly. But to be honest..." I sigh as I stand up and stretch. I pace a little bit behind the chairs.

"Talk to me, little sis."

"I'm just so nervous about everything that happened with that vile woman yesterday. I don't know what it means for me. And I really hope that Layne is okay. It's just causing me a lot of..." I flail my hands, unable to come up with the right words.

"It's upsetting. I understand. Seeing a mother slap her son like that is jarring." Matt stands after he finishes cleaning up his desk and walks over to me. He pulls me into a hug that instantly calms me. "You did the right thing. Layne is okay. He's with his dad. He went to school this morning. Desiree is in lockup right now. And all of that is because you had the balls to step in." He pulls away and looks down at me. "You really did a good thing here. I know it's fucking with your anxiety, but it's like Luca and I always tell you. It's a momentary discomfort that comes with a much greater reward."

I let out a breath. "Of course you're right."

Matt grins. "Of course I am. Need a ride home?"

"If you're not busy. Otherwise, I'll just call an Uber."

"Nah. I'm free for a bit. I wanted to swing by a house for an interview on another case anyway."

I tilt my head. "In that case? Take me home, Lieutenant Sharpe. I've had enough of the outdoors."

Matt laughs as he opens the office door. "It's Chance, you brat. Matt Sharpe? Come on."

"It sounds better." I giggle as he laughs and shakes his head. I love teasing him about taking Luca's last name, even though I know they've already agreed that it will be the other way around. Luca is taking Matt's name.

I quickly grab the lunch bag and slip out the door just in front of him as he closes and locks it.

And that is when all Hell seemingly breaks loose.

"Stop him!" someone yells.

I turn with furrowed eyebrows and see the guy who was getting escorted to lockup running down the hallway. He veers away from a couple of cops who attempt to grab him and sprints down a row of cubicles. My eyes widen, but I don't have much time to see anything else. Matt grabs my arm and almost throws me under a desk.

"Don't move," he commands.

Yeah. Right. Like there was any chance of that happening. This. This right here. This is why I don't like leaving the house. For the second day in a row, my pulse rate has reached unnatural levels, and I've been thrust into a world of chaos. I don't like chaos. I like order. A lot of it. I do not do well without it. Order is one of the greatest things about life.

I make myself as small as possible under the desk and take deep breath after deep breath. *I'm safe. It's okay. He's just one guy. There are a lot of cops here with guns. Nothing is going to happen to me.* It's a pep talk I never thought I'd have to give myself in the middle of a police station, but there it is. Me giving myself a pep talk in the middle of Gainesville Police Department's Headquarters. Command Central. One PP. Whatever they call it.

As if to make my nightmare more terrifying, because it's not scary enough, the asshat decides to run up my aisle. He can't see me from my position, but I can still see enough to be aware of what's happening. The desk I'm hiding under is at the end. I'm sure he has no idea I'm here. But come on. Seriously? Can I not catch a break? I was doing so well. I hadn't panicked at all being away from the house today.

And now I'm pissed. How dare this cockmuppet asslizard ruin my day?

No. No! He will not get the upper hand on me.

Fuck. Him.

I shove the chair in front of me away and quickly tuck myself back into my hiding place. It rolls out in front of him, and I watch in pure delight as he trips over it. He stumbles, but somehow stays upright. I let out a low growl of frustration and almost pout that he didn't go sprawling, but he's not standing for long. Matt, seemingly appearing out of nowhere, rams him like he's going in for a tackle or something. He drops to his knee and allows the guy's momentum to propel him over Matt's shoulder. The asshole lands face down on the ground with several cops surrounding him and quickly taking control back.

"Nice moves, Chance," someone says as they pat Matt on the back. "Still got some quarterback in you after all."

"Fucking asshole. Get that scum out of here," Matt says as he turns to where I am. He holds out a hand. I take it, and he pulls me up. "You okay?"

I nod and glare towards where the guy is being led off to. "I got pissed off."

Matt smiles. "Well, get pissed off more. That was some quick thinking."

"I hope that guy really does get put in with the Baiters." I shake my head and focus back on Matt.

"How the fuck do you know about the Baiters?"

I blush. "The cop who was bringing him in when I got here mentioned it after he made some leer at me about how sexy I am. He threw some kind of macho man act and said he ain't afraid of no fags," I say in my best mock asshole accent and roll my eyes. "He's an idiot that needs his eyes tested."

Matt glances back as they lead him through a door. "Huh. Maybe I'll get him thrown in there after all. Fucking with my sister isn't something I tolerate. And don't think I didn't catch that dig at yourself."

I blush. "Sorry." I shake my head. "Well, Sharpe. This has been fun, but I think I'll skip out on the rest of our lunch dates from now on."

Matt laughs. "Way to skate over the subtle warning. Let's get you home. And for fuck's sake, Luca is taking my name. Brat." He starts brushing himself off and making sure his shirt still looks presentable.

I smile, but I barely hear him because my eyes are locked on a tall man with dark hair and the sexiest jade eyes I've ever seen in my life. He's around Matt's height and built just as well. Strong. Muscular. The veins along his forearms that are just peeking out from his rolled up, forest green dress shirt make my mouth water; my throat go dry. Unlike Matt, who carries his gun in a holster attached to his hip, this man has it in a holster on his shoulder. I don't know why, but it makes him look far sexier and way more in control.

Dominant.

Dangerous.

Snapping me from whatever world he pulled me into, the man breaks eye contact and looks down at his phone as he pulls it out of his pocket. He scowls and turns, heading into an office. Matt guides me towards the garage where he parks his truck. I glance over my shoulder a few times, but the sexiest guy I have ever seen in my life has vanished behind a closed door. I have to wonder…

Did I imagine all of that?

Or did the man of my dreams, literally, really morph into reality?

Chapter Four

☆ DJ ☆

I lean my head back and close my eyes. "You're honestly asking me to bail your ass out of jail after you hit our son."

"DJ, I didn't hit him! That woman is making shit up to make me look bad. I don't even know who she is."

A low growl makes its way up my throat. "Desiree, come on. Do you really think I'm stupid? Layne corroborated everything. And I saw the fucking black eye."

"That's because she did it! She hit him! I tried to stop her."

I shake my head. "Why the hell am I still entertaining you and your lies? I'm hanging up."

"DJ, wait! I am *not* going to survive in here!"

I roll my eyes so hard I'm sure I can see the back of my own head. "You should have thought of that before you denied my damn offer. You would have been set for life, Des. I'm not helping you. I'm not bailing you out. I'm sure as fuck not putting up the house as collateral. If you'd taken my offer, you could have done that yourself instead of calling me and begging me to do it. I'm not bailing you out. Call your parents."

"Please stop being such an asshole and help me!"

I shake my head as I open my eyes. "No."

"DJ!" she squeaks out over her sobs.

I hang up and toss my cellphone on my desk. "Fuck. Why the fuck would she think to call me?" I shouldn't have answered.

But, like a fucking idiot, I did answer. And broke some intense fucking eye contact with one of the most beautiful women I've ever seen. I need to ask Matt who that woman was. All I could figure out was that she was with him. Could that have been Lyric?

Holy fuck.

Instead of introducing myself like I should have, I looked at my damn phone and disappeared into my office after answering the number for the jail. I knew it was Desiree. I walked away from a beautiful woman to talk to the one woman in the world that I'd love to string from a tree. Morbid curiosity took over. The question of why the hell she was calling me from lockup got the best of me. I needed to know the answer. I really should have fucking known already.

I look at my watch. Just after one in the afternoon. I'm more than done with this day, so I grab my gear and head for the door. I lock up behind me and stride to the garage, stopping near the receptionist for the chief on my way.

"Something came up. I'm out for the rest of the day. I'll be on my cell."

The tiny older lady smiles up at me with a nod. "Yes, sir."

I give her a smile and continue the rest of the way to the police garage where my black, convertible, Ford Mustang is parked. I get in my car and toss my gear onto the passenger seat. I start it up and smile when she purrs to life. I love my car. Driving her always centers me.

I contemplate doing just that. Taking a drive. But my mind keeps wandering to flashes of that girl and her golden hazel eyes. Then it flashes to another girl with fuck me blue eyes. I try to shake them both out of my head, but I soon find myself parking my car, grabbing my gear, and knocking on Mariah's door. Before I can snap myself out of it and walk to my own apartment, Mariah answers wearing a sexy as fuck pink tanktop and tiny jean shorts that I can't stop thinking about ripping off.

With my teeth.

"DJ?" Mariah yawns and covers her mouth. "I'm sorry. The panic hangover has set in."

Her words sober me up quickly. The craving to have her lips against mine again, her taut body underneath me, takes a backseat to the need to take care of her. She steps back and lets me in. I drop my gym bag filled with my gear, including my gun and shoulder holster, and pull her into my arms. All thoughts I had of the mystery girl diminish. The phone call with Desiree that pissed me the fuck off disappear from my mind.

"I'm sorry I had to leave like that this morning," I rumble into her hair, which I have shamelessly buried my face in. "The call was a high priority. We needed to get there and deal with it quickly before anyone vanished on us."

"I know, DJ," she says quietly into my chest as she hugs me.

"It's not. I wanted to talk to you before I left. Make sure you were okay."

The tension that had slowly been melting away since the moment I took her in my arms instantly comes back. Mariah stiffens as she takes a breath and lets go of me. She gives me a half-smile as she walks back to her couch and curls into her favorite large, white, fleece blanket. She loves it so much because it matches the decor in her apartment. I once came in with the key I have because she didn't answer the knock, even though she was the one who invited me over. I didn't see her. I almost left until I saw a glimpse of her hair peeking from underneath the blanket she had wrapped around her.

Thinking of it now, it was one of the sexiest things I've ever seen. She was dead asleep. She hadn't slept well the night before. I was late getting here because of a call that had come in that needed to be dealt with. My girl was burrowed so adorably that she took my breath away.

I watch her as I take off my shoes. For the second time since I've known her, though, Mariah refuses to look at me. The first? Last night. In my bed. I was holding her and she turned her back to me. She's never done that, and I've had her in bed after panic attacks before. Fuck, I've had her in her bed. Not once did she turn her back to me or refuse to meet my eyes the next morning.

I walk to her couch and sit next to her. Mariah keeps her eyes lowered. "Why do I get the feeling I fucked up more than I think I did?"

She gives me a soft smile. "It's not you," she says quietly. I can't help but notice that even though I've put my arm over the back of the couch, Mariah makes no motion to cuddle into my side or lay her head on my lap like she usually does. "It's the demon."

"What's he saying to you today?"

She shakes her head. "Nothing that isn't true." She lifts one shoulder in a half shrug.

My eyebrows draw together in confusion. "I'm really not following because you know the demon is a fucking liar, but I have the feeling this has something to do with me and what happened last night."

She sniffles and stands slowly. I don't move. I just watch her as she paces the room. A few times, she swipes at her eyes and sniffles, but I don't try and comfort her because I know that whatever is going on is something she needs to get out on her own terms. I know my girl well.

Damn right she's mine, the possessive motherfucker deep within me says for the millionth time since I've known her. I push him back down. This might be the first time I'm listening to him. And fucking whole-heartedly agreeing.

She starts quietly moving her lips like she's mumbling to herself. I know it's time to step in. "Rih. I'm sorry about last night. I shouldn't have…" I trail off with the next words that hit my ears.

"Not like he'd ever want me," she whispers so quietly that I nearly miss it.

I can't stop the jealousy that rises from my stomach into my chest. "Who?"

She jumps. Her head snaps towards me like she's completely forgotten I'm in the room. "What?"

I nod my head towards her as I lean forward and clasp my hands together in an attempt to keep the possessive fucking asshole at bay. I have no claim to her. No right to be pissed off that she may or may not be interested in someone. But dammit, I'm fucking seething.

"You. You just said 'not like he'd ever want me.' I want to know who."

Her cheeks flame an instant red. She puts her hands to her face to cover and shakes her head. "Nothing. It's nothing."

"I know you better than that. It is something. Whatever is going on with you is definitely something." Suddenly, as if I'm the Wicked Witch of the West, and she's Dorothy dropping a house on my head, everything becomes clear. "Oh fuck." I lean back against the couch, stunned. "This.

All of this. The panic attack. This thing that's happening right now. It all has to do with last night. You're spiraling because of my reaction. Not the actual actions. And it's even worse because I said I shouldn't have done it."

She bites her lip and looks down. She says nothing at all, but she doesn't have to. I get it now. I kissed her. I fucking dry humped her until we both made a mess of ourselves. And then I ran out of here so quickly in my own fucking panic that I thought nothing of her. I caused her to not only panic, but get sucked into the fucking darkness that she tries so hard to avoid that lives in her head. I bolted and left her with her demon filling her mind with all of the bullshit she's thinking right now that isn't true.

Then in order to attempt and relax herself, she took a shower because it has a massage spray setting. But with her demon shouting nonsense at her, she didn't think for a second that a shower wouldn't be a good idea in the slightest. It caused an even bigger attack which sent her directly to me. The one person in her life who has always been at her side, and then fucking ran from her when she needed him the most.

"Rih, come here, baby. Please. We need to talk." I hold out a hand for her and let her come to me. I know her well enough to know that sudden moves will send her into a panic. It all has to do with her past.

Mariah takes a breath and slowly comes towards me. She shakily takes my hand and begins to move to my side, but I'm not having it. I pull her down so she's straddling me. She stares at me with wide eyes as she braces her hands on my shoulders. I've had her in my lap. I've held her tightly. I've cuddled with her. But not once have either of us found ourselves in this position. I've never had her straddle me like this. It was completely for myself. I couldn't have her like this because I wouldn't be able to fight my feelings for her.

I wrap my arms around her and pull her as close to me as I can while I look into those gorgeous eyes. They say a person can see another person's soul through their eyes. I don't know if that's true, but what I see in hers is every emotion going through her beautiful mind. Confusion. Wonder. A little bit of sadness. Something akin to happiness.

But above everything else… hope.

It's the hope that fucking floors me.

"Tell me what happened last night," I say dominantly as I always do when I want information. Or a confirmation of it.

"It's not your fault… It's mine."

I shake my head. "No. It isn't. Tell me what happened. I kissed you. I made you come. I made a mess of us both. I bolted. What happened after that? Up until you ended up having one of the worst attacks I've seen."

"DJ, I… can't…"

I run my fingers through her hair, knowing I'm going to have to start this conversation. She'll shut down on me otherwise. "I'm sorry, Rih."

She shakes her head and looks down. "Don't. I fought myself so hard yesterday. I know you're not ready for a relationship. I know you don't even want one. I know you. And even if you did, it definitely wouldn't be with me. We're friends. And we're friends for a reason. I'm the complete opposite of the women you like."

I can't help but chuckle at that. I tend to go for blonds with blue eyes. Women who, in Mariah's very words plenty of times, look like Barbie. She has teased me about it. It's a sentiment that I've never disagreed with because she's right. I've never married a woman with curves of any kind. Most look like supermodels and really are the opposite of Mariah.

I've always thought she was just joking with me. I was stupid. It's all so fucking clear now. Her teasing digs were never just her fucking with me. They were subtle reminders that there is a woman right in front of me who loves me. And even though she's the opposite of the others, she's still here. Right here.

Fuck. So conceited of me. Arrogant. Dumb.

"Mariah, I need to be honest here. Just because you aren't leggy and blond, doesn't mean for a second that you're not attractive." I hold a finger to her lips when she opens her mouth to say something. "And it doesn't mean that I'm not attracted to you." I slowly lower my finger and sigh when she presses her pretty lips together. "Last night, well, it was a fucking mistake on my part. I ran off because I do have feelings for you. Feelings that I was afraid to admit to myself because I didn't want to fuck up what we have. You're my best friend, Rih. You're so nonjudgmental. You're sweet. You listen to me bitch about my day and actually understand me in ways no one else does. Not even Matt. I love that. I love it so much that losing it because of the feelings I have for you gives me anxiety. I don't want to mess things up. But I realized something." I pause and watch her as my words sink further and further into her. "You are *everything* I've ever wanted in a woman. When I kissed you last night, all of those feelings I never thought I'd have for anyone came rushing to the surface. It scared the hell out of me because it's shit I've always felt for you. No one else."

She closes her eyes slowly and tilts her head back. She lets out a breath as she relaxes more and more into me. "Me too."

I tangle my fingers in her hair and lean forward a little. I close my eyes as I breathe her in and kiss her throat. "I made you come because I couldn't stop myself. I knew it was about to happen. It shocked me a little bit because of how quickly it came on, but I could have pulled back. I didn't because I wanted to be the only one whose ever done it. And I followed right behind you because of how pretty you were when you did it. I panicked and ran. I didn't think of you, and that was the mistake. The only mistake. I don't regret for a second that I kissed you or that either of us came afterwards. I'm done fighting it. I want you, Rih. Last night wasn't enough to satisfy my craving for you." I kiss along her throat to her neck.

"DJ...," she whispers.

I smile against her neck and kiss up to her jaw. "Tell me what happened last night. I need to know." I don't stop leaving soft kisses. I keep one hand tangled in her hair. The other, I rub up and down the length of her back.

"The demon. He just taunted me," she says breathily and quietly.

"Tell me." I move to the other side of her face and kiss down to her neck.

Her fingers shakily grip my shoulders, and she sniffles, but she tilts her head to the side, allowing me more access to her delicious skin. I take the liberty of licking it with a quiet rumble of possession before I kiss where I licked. I suck lightly.

She shivers. "He kept... mmm... saying we'd never happen. I'm... DJ..." she arches into me when I nip where I was sucking. I smile and tangle her hair around my fist. I let the other fall to her ass and squeeze it. She presses down on my hardening cock, making it twitch for her.

"Then what?" I whisper in her ear while I let her press herself down on me more.

With still shaky hands, she runs one through my hair. "I'm not good enough. Pretty enough. That you'll never want me."

I shake my head slowly and meet her lips with a gentle kiss that shoots sparks through my entire body. I pull away slowly. "Your demon can go fuck himself. Because none of that is true. I do want you. I have since the second I saw you, Rih. But you've always been different. You've always been special to me. The closer you and I got, the more I realized that not only are you good enough, but you're way too good for me. Not only are you pretty enough, you're way above my league. And not only do I want you, I need you. So much it physically hurts sometimes. I never wanted to ruin what I have with you. So, I kept all of those feelings locked up tight. I don't want to do that anymore. I can't. Not since I gave into them. I can't put them back now."

"I don't know how long I've wanted to hear you say those words," she whispers against my lips.

And I'm done.

She doesn't know what she's doing. I'm sure of it. But the way she's moving over me has me so hard for her that I'm close to busting through the zipper of my black slacks.

Thankfully, I'm not the only one. Much like last night, Mariah is losing control, and it's fucking sexy as hell to watch. She's grinding against my zipper. Instead of stopping it and making her talk, I let her take what she needs as I groan in appreciation and hug her tighter.

It doesn't take long for the intensity of the kisses to take over. Both of my hands have fallen to her perfect ass and I'm pressing her down on me as I push into her. She whimpers, but it's obvious she's not getting the relief she needs this time. Even though she's grinding harder against me than she was last night. I'm going straight to hell because I'm fucking letting her. Encouraging it.

"DJ...," she whispers. It's more of a plea. For what, I don't know.

Keeping one arm tightly around her, I slide the other one over her thigh. Thanks to the short as hell shorts, her thigh is pretty much fully exposed. Which means getting to the part of her that's yearning for me and driving my dick insane is easy.

I don't even hesitate. It feels right, so it can't be wrong, can it? Is she going to slap me for this? The questions race through my mind, but I push her panties and the crotch of her shorts aside anyway. And when I push my middle finger inside her, all of those questions fade away because, holy Christ, my girl is wet.

For me.

I groan as I thrust my finger inside her. Her eyes widen in shock, but I can see the heat in them; feel it between her thighs. Her body trembles for me. Her pussy tightens as I thrust. I kiss her neck and let her hold on for the ride I'm taking her on. Her pussy pulses for me as she gets even wetter.

"Fuck, baby," I rumble against her sweet skin. "I cannot wait to taste you." I thrust harder as she lets out a squeak at my words and tightens even more as she rides my finger.

I refrain from adding a second because she's way too tight and too close to her breaking point. So instead, I crook my middle finger against the spot inside her that I know will get her to crumble for me. I set my thumb against her clit and start rubbing.

"Oh! Oh… God…" She collapses right there. Her pussy clenches repeatedly as she comes.

"Jesus Christ, sexy girl," I growl against her neck as she buries her face in my shoulder and whimpers. I slow my thrusts and rubs to help her come down and grin against her neck. "Less than a minute. I think that's a new record for me."

"DJ!" she swats my arm as I laugh.

I slowly pull my finger out of her pretty pussy and right her panties and shorts. As she pants against me, I suck her off my finger with a groan. "My Christ, you taste even more incredible than I imagined."

She looks at me, confused, then squeaks again and hides when she sees what I'm doing. "DJ!"

I laugh and wrap her back in my arms. I hold her for I don't even know how long before I decide we need to finish the talk we started.

"What happened after that? What made you think to take a shower?"

She slumps in my arms. I hate that I have to ask the question, especially after bringing her to that high, but I need to know. I know she hates showers. I know all of the reasons why. She has a jacuzzi tub for a reason. It's right next to her small, stand-up shower, and she had it specially installed.

"I wanted to relax," she whispers and shakes her head. "I was just thinking about the massage setting on the showerhead. The jets in the jacuzzi are nice, but they don't reach between my shoulders… I carry so much tension and stress there. I didn't even know how much time had passed from when you walked out the door to when I went to the shower. It was hours. I felt like it was minutes. I thought I'd be okay. I really do love that showerhead. And usually, I am okay if I have music on and don't close my eyes. But the music cut out. Or paused. Something. I don't know." She sniffles and shakes her head again.

I hug her tighter, subtly giving her the encouragement she needs to continue. "I got you," I whisper.

She tries to move off my lap, but I don't let her. I lock my arms around her tighter. She watches me curiously before she takes a breath. "I closed my eyes. I don't remember doing that. The demon started in on me. Yelling that he was behind me. I turned. He wasn't. But the demon kept saying he was. And then, I saw Robert." She bites her lip and finally gives into wrapping her arms around me. She buries her face in my neck.

Robert.

The fucker who molested her repeatedly when she was a child. If I ever get my hands on him, he's dead. I, unfortunately, know he's not. I know he lives in fucking Kerrick, Minnesota. I know he's alive and well. I'm not even going to pretend like I'm not keeping my eyes on the son of a bitch. It's an abuse of power, but if he ever moves from that area to anywhere in the country, I'll know because I have an alert set up on him.

"At first, that's how it was. The usual. The demon screaming that he was behind me. Me looking to see that he wasn't. But it was a little different this time because I was past the point of being terrified before I even saw his shadow. Then, I saw his silhouette. And he kept screaming that Robert was behind me. Even when I got out and got to my safeplace. My chair in the corner of the living room by the window. Even when I got there, the demon wouldn't stop. I ran to you. You were all I could think of that makes it stop and makes me feel safe. But when I got to your door, the demon kept saying I was stupid for bothering you."

My heart actually swells that she came to me when she needed to feel safe. Even though this all started because of me. I sway gently with her. I press my lips against her neck. "You're always safe with me, baby. Always. And you're never ever a bother to me. The demon was wrong again. And Robert is never getting to you. So, he was wrong about that, too."

"I wish I wasn't like this. I always feel psychotic after panic like that."

"Baby." I tug her hair a little so she's looking at me. When she does, I kiss her. "PTSD isn't something to fuck around with. I still, to this very day, have to sleep facing the door. And it has to be cool, or I have to have a fan on. If I don't, I get taken right back to my time in the Middle East. A time where I had to sleep with one eye open and facing the door to our tent or barracks because if I didn't and someone snuck in on me or my team, it meant life or death. I have to have that air on me at night. If I don't, I think of how hot things were there. Which makes me think of everything else that happened. Fireworks. I can handle them, but those initial loud booms send my heart rate into the stratosphere. You were in a traumatic situation, Rih."

"I know," she says quietly. "I just wish I could get over it."

"You don't just get over it. You work through it. You find ways to cope. And you do very well. The music being on when you do take showers. It's a way for you to push through it. But it doesn't change the fact that the reason you have issues with closing your eyes in the shower is because your eyes were closed when he attacked you and assaulted you in the shower. And it doesn't change the fact that you always have to have a fan on, no matter how cold you are, when you sleep because he attacked you and held a pillow over your head while he assaulted you in the middle of the night. You do things, even subconsciously, just like I do, to cope with things you don't even remember happening until those repressed memories come back and slap you. You do all you can to survive. You have to give yourself credit for that, sweet girl."

She smiles softly, though tears fill her eyes. Nothing I've told her is anything different than what I've told her in the past. But it's all things I'll tell her every single day if she needs me to. Anything to bring her back down and realize how incredible she is.

"Thank you," she whispers as she rests her forehead against mine.

I kiss her again because I'm incapable of resisting her lips. "What about you and I head over to my apartment? I'll start dinner. Layne is staying with his boyfriend, Beckett, for the weekend. They have some huge science project due. You and I can have a quiet night in." I smile. "I'll even let you pick the movie."

Her soft smile brightens a little. "Barbecue chicken?" she asks hopefully.

I grin. "I'll fire up the grill on the balcony."

She brightens a little more. "With grilled corn on the cob?"

"Anything you want."

"And *The Day After Tomorrow* for the movie?"

"Whatever my girl wants. I'll even do potato salad and watermelon balls. I just bought one last night." I know she loves when I scoop watermelon out of the rind instead of cutting it into triangles. She's never eaten it like that before, but it's easier, less messy, and makes her happy.

"Then, yes. I'd love to."

I laugh. "Are you trying to tell me…" I trail off as I shift her a little. I stand with her in my arms. She giggles and wraps her legs around my waist and arms around my shoulders. I lean in and kiss her with a low groan as I walk to her door. I smile when I pull away. I lean down to grab my gear and open her door. "That you wouldn't have agreed to my date night if one or more of those things were missing?"

She giggles as I close her door and lock it, then walk towards my apartment. "Yep."

I laugh. "I'm glad we talked."

She smiles and rubs her nose along mine. "Me too," she whispers.

I kiss her again and keep my lips locked on hers while I let us into my apartment. I explore her mouth as I close the door behind me. I drop my gear on the floor and don't stop kissing her even when I get to my couch. I nip and suck on her tongue, unable to pull away, as I lay down, settling her on top of me.

She grinds into me, though I'm sure she's just moving the way she feels is natural. She's doing nothing but turning us both on. My dick gets harder and harder. Her nipples turn to pebbles that I can feel through the thin fabric of both of our shirts. She feels so fucking good. It feels right. Is it too soon? I really should stop this before it goes to my bedroom because I'm not sure either of us are ready for that yet. I've already had her once today. I should go start that chicken.

But I don't…

Chapter Five

☆ Mariah ☆

I really should stop. Are we going too far? It feels so right. I sink further and further into DJ. I've never in my life been kissed so passionately. So deeply. So intensely. So all consumingly. Is that a word? I don't know. I don't even care. The only thing on my mind is DJ's tongue dominating mine. His hands all over me. Everywhere at the same time.

I push myself against him. He pushes into me and deepens the kiss. I didn't know it could get any better, but he takes it to a whole other level. He drives my desire for him to a place I'm unfamiliar with. A place I've never been taken before by anyone but him. He's the only one I've ever been with who has made me come. I've never lost control like I have with him. I've never felt comfortable enough to let anyone but him have it.

DJ sits up slowly. Keeping his arms around me and not breaking the kiss, he lifts me with him and carries me down the hallway. He enters his bedroom and kicks the door closed. All the while, his tongue is doing things to me I've never experienced. I was married once. Kissing never felt this good. Nothing ever felt this good with anyone other than DJ.

He drops me on the bed and climbs on top of me. "Tell me to stop." He kisses down my neck and nips just below my jaw. "I will. Just say the words." His voice sends some kind of delicious vibrations throughout my whole body.

I close my eyes as I sigh and shiver. I shake my head and grip him tighter. "No," I whisper.

I let my body lead me. It's telling me that I'm ready for this. That I need him as much as everything he wants to give me. I'll greedily accept all of it. I kiss his stubbled jaw, down to his shoulder, and grip his shirt. He presses his hips into mine. I gasp. I've never felt anything like him. I've been with two men in my life. Neither of them were near where he is in size. His dick drives me crazy with an insatiable need.

I push his shirt up. DJ takes the control he loves and breaks the kiss only long enough to sit up on his knees. Without unbuttoning the shirt more than a couple of buttons, he pulls it off and tosses it. I reach for his belt and start undoing it as he cages me underneath him once more. His lips crash to mine again, awakening parts of me I was sure died long ago. Parts of me only he's ever managed to reach.

As I fumble with his belt and button on his pants, DJ expertly undoes mine with one flick. I can feel his smirk against my lips as my eyes widen, and I squeak. I don't need to see the cockiness in his eyes, but I'm glad I do. I love DJ's eyes, but when they're dancing with humor, they become even more unique and bright.

As I fight his zipper, DJ starts kissing down my collarbone. When he gets to the peaks of my nipples over my tank top and bra, he nips. I gasp and arch into him, tugging his zipper towards me instead of down.

DJ grins. "That's not going to help you get them off, baby." He nips the other nipple.

"Oh!" I tug him towards me again. "DJ, you're impossible."

He laughs. "Judging completely by your body language, I'm gonna go out on a limb and say you love it."

I whimper when he sits up on his knees again. It means his body isn't against mine. His lips aren't doing things to me that no one else ever has. He grips my shorts and tugs them down roughly with my panties. He tosses them wherever his shirt went and dives between my legs with his tongue.

"Ah!" I cry out bucking wildly into him. One hand automatically finds his hair. The other tangles in the comforter below me. "DJ!"

"Yes?" he growls as he flicks his tongue back and forth and sucks. Hard.

I can't say a word. All I can do is moan and thrash underneath him. No one has ever gone down on me. No one has ever managed to send me into some dark abyss of pleasure with a simple touch. My entire body feels like it's jerking and quaking underneath him as he relentlessly licks, sucks, and thrusts his tongue into me.

"Oh…," I finally manage to groan out as my eyes fall closed, and I completely give into him.

"Fuck, Rih. You don't know how many times I've dreamed of this. You taste much sweeter in person than I could ever dream."

I have no time to unpack what that means because that tongue is swirling inside me like a tornado. The literal definition of a tongue twister. And once again, just when I think it can't get better, DJ one ups himself and drives me even more crazy. He licks, nips, and sucks up to my clit. He shoves two fingers into me. Not just one like he had not long before. Something must be wrong with me because I greedily accept him.

He thrusts hard and deep but slow enough so that I feel all of him. Every single callus on his fingers. He sucks that sweet little bud into his mouth and devours it while he crooks his fingers as I arch and buck into him.

"Oh God… DJ… Please… Please…" My pussy pulses erratically. I writhe under him. I know I'm close to the peak I've only ever brought myself before him. It feels so much better when he does it.

"Please? Please what?" he teases.

I scratch and grip the blanket. My whole body is trembling. My pussy is on the verge of exploding. "I'm…," I pant.

"I'm… what?" He thrusts faster and twists his fingers.

My eyes fly open. My stomach tightens and clenches as tight as my pussy. "I'm gonna come!"

"Good girl," he rumbles against me. "Come, baby girl. Give me all of you," he commands. No one has ever told me to come, but oh my God do I love when he does it.

I stare at him in shock when he stays between my legs. He continues pumping his fingers in and out of me at a pace that brings me further and further to my breaking point. He doesn't stop licking and sucking on my clit.

I buck into him until my climax hits me like a speeding train. "Ah!" I scream. I slap a hand over my mouth with wide eyes as my pussy clenches tight around his fingers and spasms. "DJ!" I scream into my hand.

He moans low and thrusts slowly as he licks me tenderly and lovingly. "Fuck, Mariah. You're so beautiful when you lose all control like that. I'm never going to get tired of watching you break for me."

I lay motionless, enjoying his soothing caresses and gentle strokes as he brings me down from my second high of the day. From somewhere no one but him is aware I've never been to with anyone else. I try to catch my breath as I fall.

Or at least feel like I am.

When I come back to myself, DJ is lying next to me tracing patterns on my stomach. He's pushed my tank top up to my breasts, but hasn't exposed them. I let my eyes wander down his body slowly when I feel something hard pushing against my side.

I blink a few times. I've imagined what he looks like underneath his clothes, but the DJ in front of me and the DJ in my mind are two so very different things. I've seen him with no shirt. I know how muscular he is. He has lickable abs and muscles I'd love nothing more than to trace... with my tongue. One could bounce a quarter off his ass.

But it's the thick, long, hard rod of steel jutting out from a well-groomed nether region that has my mouth watering. I've felt him between my legs. I came last night after grinding against him. But not once have I seen him fully exposed to me like this before.

My pussy clenches as if he's already inside me. I've imagined it, but I've never seen anyone as big as he is in anything other than porn videos, which I'm not ashamed to admit I used to get myself off with my trusty, purple or pink bullet. Yes. I have two. And a dildo, which I've only used twice.

"When did your pants come off?" I whisper. I immediately blush. "That wasn't how I wanted that to sound."

DJ grins and leans down. He hovers with his lips just grazing mine. "You mean adorable?"

I blush darker. "That wasn't adorable. That was... odd. And weird. Obviously, it happened while I was coming down from the best orgasm of my life."

DJ laughs. "You think that was the best orgasm of your life? Man, I'm gonna have a lot of fun with you."

I hide my face in my hands. "Stop. How do the orgasms keep getting better? We've hardly done anything." I laugh and feel him shift. I peek through my fingertips at him. Once again, he's between my legs. Only this time, he's pulling me up with him.

"I'm not even close to being done with you. I need that wet pussy wrapped around my cock."

My eyes widen as he pulls my shirt up. "So, everything is bigger in Texas, and Texas guys have a dirtier mouth in the bedroom?" I tease.

He throws his head back and laughs. "Well, we ain't in Texas, honey," he says, playing up his Southern accent. "I ain't been there for years. But as for things being bigger..." He trails off and looks down at his erection with a shrug and smirk. "Maybe. I definitely am. I can confirm we for sure have a dirtier mouth."

His lips meet mine in a fiery kiss that fuels a need for him that will never be quenched. I let him unhook my bra and pull it off. I don't know where it goes because he's pushing me back on the bed and covering me with his body.

"DJ..." I wrap my arms around his shoulders and spread my legs wide as I hook my feet behind his knees. "I've never felt so needy as I do right now. I honestly feel like some horny girl who can't get enough satisfaction and just needs more and more and more. I hate how it makes me feel so dirty and..." I trail off, not knowing how to express myself as I look into his jade eyes. It's like they're piercing my soul.

I feel the head of his cock against me. If I arched enough, he'd slide right in. "I don't think that makes you needy or dirty." He leans in and kisses me softly as he thrusts his entire dick into me hard.

My nails dig into his back. "Mmm!"

"All it tells me is that you've never had a man who treated you right." He starts moving, slowly, but thrusts deeply. "It means you've experienced something you haven't, and you want more." He kisses across my jaw to my ear. "And I'm happy to give you all you want," he whispers. "Over..." He punctuates the word with a hard thrust. Slow enough that I feel each and every ridge as my pussy stretches around him. "And over..." Another hard thrust. "And... over..." One more hard thrust.

My head falls back. "DJ!"

"Fuck, I love my name on your lips." He pulls all the way out and thrusts all the way back in. Deep. I pant and arch into his thrusts. He kisses his way to my neck and takes advantage of my throat bared to him. I'm starting to think it's his favorite place to kiss.

I moan into his shoulder and pull him closer to me. He wraps one arm around me and lifts my hip with the other, so he sinks deeper. It causes me to gasp, but then he rolls his hips, and I can't formulate words or cohesive thoughts. All I can think of is him.

His completely masculine and earthy scent.

The ridges of his muscles working as he thrusts into me.

Each and every inch of his velvet encased cock pumping in and out of me.

"Open your eyes, Rih," he whispers. I vaguely hear him make the demand. My body obeys on its own.

"Oh my…, DJ… Fuck…, you feel so good…" I'm so tight around him. Or maybe it's just that he's so big. I don't know. He makes me feel like I'm not even in this world anymore.

He keeps his eyes on me and takes one hardened nipple into his mouth. He sucks as he picks up the pace with his thrusts. My thighs tighten around his hips. My pussy feels like it's pulling him in with each and every thrust. I get wetter and wetter. Tighter and tighter. DJ gets harder and harder. Thicker and thicker.

He moves his mouth to my other nipple and nips it. I arch into his mouth. His eyes never leave mine. "I want your eyes open. I want to watch every emotion that plays out in your eyes when I make you come again." He takes my nipple into his mouth once more and sucks.

I fight against closing my eyes as waves of ecstasy wash over me. I meet his thrusts until we both are moving together at a feverish pace. I feel myself tightening around him as my stomach begins to clench. My pussy pulses uncontrollably once more, but I don't want him to stop.

Not yet.

"So good. DJ, fuck… You feel so good. So big. Thick." I hold onto him as tightly as I can.

"So…fucking… tight…"

His hips rock against mine. He slams into me. I never thought I'd like hard, rough sex, but apparently DJ did because he's giving me everything I need and didn't know I did. And then he's surpassed that and given me so, so much more.

Our skin slaps against each other's. The sound of my pussy taking his cock is dirty. Primal. Nothing I've ever heard before, but it spurs me on. I spread my legs wider and move them up so they're locked around his waist.

"Oh… fuck…, baby…," he groans against my chest, his dick sinking impossibly deeper.

My eyes widen when he starts pounding my pussy faster. It makes me clench tighter around him. Once again, as he brings me to my precipice, my entire body feels like it's shaking as hard and fast as my pussy is. He kisses up to my neck. I tangle my fingers in his hair and pull him into me. I kiss him hard and pray that he knows I'm about to come, because I don't think I can say anything.

Does he feel me come? How does that work? I know when his fingers were inside me I clenched and tightened and pulsed, but can he feel that? Is that stupid and naive of me to think?

I won't hold on much longer. Can I come before he does? Is that allowed? I wish I was more experienced. What forty-year-old has only had sex with two men for a grand total of like fifteen times in her entire life between the two of them?

"Get out of your head, Rih," DJ rumbles against my neck.

"Oh…," I moan as his voice slams me back into reality. Moaning is all I can do because he feels so good. "I'm…" I cling to him and buck up into him, willing him to understand that I'm there. "I can't…" I can't form a sentence. That's what I can't do. "I can't…" I can't hold on. "DJ!"

He smiles against my neck and kisses up to my lips. Looking deep into my eyes, his own on fire, he lowers his lips to mine. "Come. Squeeze my cock. Give me what I want."

My eyes roll back into my head. I clamp down around him and scream. "Ah! DJ, fuck me!" I wrap around him tighter because he's the only thing anchoring me. I bite his shoulder and moan. My walls collapse around him. My hips jerk into his. My pussy spasms as my stomach clenches. "Ah!" I scream into his shoulder.

He starts to pull out, but I keep him held as tightly as possible as I continue orgasming around him. "Fuck, Mariah. I'm gonna come."

"Don't… please…," I whimper as I try to keep him as close as possible.

It's his turn to stare at me in shock. His dick is pulsing and throbbing. I can feel it. "What?"

"I need to feel you… please…" I know he's had a vasectomy. He told me. I can't have kids, but it's something I haven't quite been able to admit yet to anyone because it's something that makes me feel like a failure. Completely irrational, and I know it's my demon getting to me, but it's one thing I can't fight off.

"Jesus, Mariah." He kisses me long and deeply again, tangling his tongue with mine as he thrusts a couple of more times. Hard. Deep. So deep. He buries himself in me and comes so hard, I'm certain he's filling my stomach.

I clench around him again and hold him as tightly as possible as I come a second time, triggered by how good he feels. He's like nothing I've ever felt and everything I've ever wanted all at once.

After several minutes of staying connected and holding each other, DJ finally pulls out. I whimper a little at the loss but realize very quickly that it's for the best. I honestly feel like a virgin who was fucked for the very first time.

DJ pulls me to his side as he chuckles. "Looks like we finished just in time for dinner. That might be a good thing. We'll need the energy."

I giggle and snuggle into him. "I'm honestly not sure I can handle another round. I'm pretty sure I'll feel you inside me for days."

DJ grins and kisses me softly as his fingers gently rub the back of my neck. "Good. That means I did my job."

I blush. "I've never… Not… Fuck, DJ… No one but you has ever… made…" I shake my head, unable to articulate the words I want to.

DJ chuckles. "I know, baby."

I burrow into him. "So…, what now?"

He hugs me close and tight. I close my eyes and sink into him, unsure where we go from here. "Now? I'm not going to be able to let you go, Mariah. You're everything I've ever wanted. You're strong, passionate, creative, talented as hell, smart as fuck. There's no going back. I need you."

A thought occurs to me suddenly. I gasp, even as my heart seemingly flies away with the promise in his words. "What about Desiree?"

He shrugs. "This will be over soon enough. Until then, I guess we have to keep saying we're nothing more than friends."

"What if she calls me back up to the stand for some stupid reason and her lawyer asks me again what I am to you."

DJ is quiet for a long time, but he keeps me close to him. He runs his fingers through my hair and kisses my forehead periodically as he thinks about the ramifications of what's happening right now. I stay quiet because I know DJ well enough to know that he has to figure it out before he'll say a word.

Finally, he takes a deep breath and tugs my hair lightly. "We'll just have to cross that bridge if it comes."

I nod and push all of the thoughts running through my head away. After several more minutes of lying in his arms, DJ finally gets up. After we get cleaned up and dressed, he starts cooking dinner. I watch him, and we laugh and joke. We fall into the same routine that is so familiar and comfortable to us. Only now, there's a lot more touching and flirting and soft kisses. It's all so natural. Like we're not trying to hide our feelings from each other.

Not that we were dancing around each other before. We weren't. We just have nothing at all to hold back now. It feels right. Peaceful.

But even as he cuddles me close after we eat, and I snuggle into him to watch my favorite movie, I can't stop the demon whispering in the back of my head. No matter how much I try to shut him up, he's there.

He'll get sick of you, he whispers.

I close my eyes. *No, he won't. He hasn't yet.*

I can feel the demon chuckle. Like he knows something I don't. I shiver. DJ holds me closer and pulls the blanket we're wrapped in up higher, but the cold is deep. Penetrating.

What if he really does get sick of me? I ask myself. I burrow myself closer, gripping the waistband of his sweats. *I won't survive that.*

"Hey, my girl's demon. You need to get this through your fucking head," he whispers in my ear. My eyes widen at him talking directly to the fictional demon that cuts me down daily. "I'm... not... going... anywhere... I'm in this for the long haul."

And just like that, everything is okay again. It's like his words made the demon burst into flames while, at the same time, filling me with all of the confidence I need.

In him.

In myself.

In us.

Chapter Six

☆ Lyric ☆

(Three Months Later)

"Ready for this?" my brother, Luca, asks me.

I glance at him, then return my eyes to the door of the courtroom in front of me. I'm wearing a blue long-sleeve shirt that has buttons that I've buttoned halfway and rolled the sleeves up on. I have a black vest underneath it and skinny denim jeggings. If I have to go out, I usually take something that smells like Matt or my brother because it's comforting to me and calms my nerves.

This shirt, though, doesn't smell like either of them. Matt has a very spicy scent. Not overpowering, but definitely something that shows he's in charge. Luca is a lot more subtle. Like a fresh rain or something. This scent calms me so much more than either of them. It's spicy, yet subtle. Earthy, yet musky. Strong and dominant, yet safe and enveloping. It might sound crazy, but it's how I've always dreamt my ideal partner would smell. The love of my life.

I let out a breath and shake my head. The wonders of being pansexual. Attracted to a woman I've never met and a scent belonging to a man I've never seen. At least I don't think I have. If it belongs to one of Matt's and Luca's friends, and it has to because it doesn't belong to either one of them, then it has to someone I've never seen. I tend to stay hidden when they have people over. Several more things about me that make me fairly certain I'm not normal. Attracted to a woman online, a scent, and I never talk to anyone. Yeah. So normal.

"It's not that I don't want to help." I pull at the ends of the shirt. "It's… that…"

Luca rubs his hand up and down my back. "That you don't want to be here. You're not comfortable being around so many people. That even though you wouldn't change what led you here, you also wish it never happened in the first place. Both because Layne would never have been hurt, and also because you could stay in your safe bubble."

I smile softly. "No one seems to understand that," I say a little sadly. "I try really hard to get out of it, but it's not easy for me. I think, other than you and Matt, the only person who has ever understood in all of my thirty-one years of existence, is Mariah."

Luca hugs me to his side and sways gently. "I don't think we're the only three people in the world who get it."

"Probably not. But you're the only three people in my circle. Therefore, no one else exists," I joke.

Luca laughs quietly. There's no one else in this area. Voices echo just as loudly as shoes. Which, by the way, should never be heels. I make a face at the woman who steps off the elevator with smart business attire and a briefcase. And heels. Heels that I'm fairly certain add seven inches to her already too tall height.

She disappears into a courtroom, and I'm actually really grateful that it wasn't into the one I'm supposed to be in. She had to be over six feet in those heels. She already gave off an air of intimidation. The height only adds to the entire atmosphere surrounding her.

I let out another long breath. "Can we just get this over with?"

"When they're ready for you, the bailiff will come out and call you in. Don't worry. I'll be there with you. Matt will already be in there and will stay in there. You'll be okay. Matt ran you through practice questions. So did DJ's attorney. You aced them. And you can keep your eyes on me and Matt the whole time."

"It's so scary," I whisper and look back down on my sneakers.

"I know. But you know you have support in there. You won't be alone. And you know that DJ's attorney is vicious. So, he won't let Desiree's attorney get away with anything."

"You know, I feel bad that I've never met him now." I sniffle. "I wish I could've just convinced myself to stay downstairs while you were watching the game." I shake my head. "He probably thinks I'm a freak or something."

"Lily… No. He doesn't think that at all. You'd be surprised at just how much he understands you. His girlfr-"

"Ms. Sharpe. We're ready for you," the Bailiff says as he opens the door.

Luca helps me up, and we make our way into the courtroom. There aren't many people in here. On Desiree's side, there are a couple of older people and a younger woman sitting behind her in the pews. Probably her parents and a friend or sibling or something.

On the other side, Matt is sitting next to Beckett, Matt's adopted son and Layne's boyfriend, Layne, who is sitting next to Beckett and holding his hand, and another woman that I don't know, who is sitting at Matt's side. They are all behind a man and his attorney. The man must be DJ, but I have a sudden feeling of deja vu. I haven't seen the man's face yet, but I feel like I know him. Other than the few people, the court reporter, the judge, and the bailiff, there's no one else.

This is a good thing.

Luca sits on the other side of the woman as I make my way to the front where I'm sworn in. I keep my eyes lowered until I'm seated because I need to focus my mind on anything other than the panic rising into my throat. I'm beyond nervous.

Tell the truth. That's all you need to do.

Matt's words play on repeat in my mind until I'm calm enough to look up as DJ's attorney, Mr. Anderson, clears his throat and begins to stand. The questioning is about to begin. All I have to do is say what happened. Nothing more. Nothing less.

And then my eyes meet his.

Those beautiful jade eyes that melted me when I first saw them.

I didn't know who they belonged to then. Just some cop who worked with Matt. Not to say I didn't dream of them every single night. Or fantasize about the man they belong to every single day. I never in an infinite number of years believed that those eyes belong to the man sitting in front of me.

DJ Rens. Father of Layne Rens.

I've never seen DJ. At least I didn't believe I had.

But I did. DJ is one of the two people in this world I dream of. I feel it in my heart, though I've never seen his face in my dreams. Not until that day at the police station. I had a face to the man I dreamt of, but didn't know my connection to him. Not until today.

Luca was cut off out there, but he was about to say girlfriend. Of course someone like him has a girlfriend. Was I completely insane for believing for a second that someone like me had a shot in Hell with a man like him? Of course I was. He's so clearly out of my league that he would probably find it hilarious to know I was interested in him.

His girlfriend's probably the totally gorgeous woman sitting behind him.

That long, beautiful hair up in a sexy bun. Blue eyes that anyone would drown in. That soft smile. I recognize it. She's the other person I've never seen the face of in my dreams. But it's her. I feel it in my heart.

My heart that's crumbling in my chest.

The woman might be trying to be discreet, but it's clear how much she cares for him in the way she looks at him when no one else is watching. I would never stand a chance. I mentally berate myself for even considering being in either of their leagues for a second.

I shake my head and fight back the tears. That's a battle for another day. Right now, my job is to help Layne. And DJ. Everything Layne, Matt, and Luca have told me about him shows what an incredible father and man he is.

"Ms. Sharpe," Mr. Anderson begins. I can't remember his first name. Another thing to berate myself for. My memory with names is terrible. Actually, it sucks full stop. It's a wonder I even remember what happened to Layne. "Will you state your name and spell it for the record please?"

"Lyric Lily Sharpe. First name is L-y-r-i-c. Middle name is L-i-l-y. Last name is S-h-a-r-p-e."

"Thank you, Ms. Sharpe. I called you here today because of an incident occurring on September the twelfth of this year. Can you tell us what that incident was?"

"Yes, sir." I try to focus on Matt and Luca, but my eyes keep straying to DJ and the woman sitting behind him. They both make my stomach flip and my heart quicken while simultaneously making me want to run away. I clear my throat and swallow. "I was on my morning walk. I heard some arguing coming from a house not too far from where I live. I walk by it every single day. I've heard arguing a lot. This time, I saw Layne, he's the boy who lives there, coming out of the house. He looked upset. I saw…" I trail off, unsure what I was supposed to call her. "Um…" I close my eyes and take a steadying breath. "Um… I saw Mrs. Rens following him outside. She was shrieking at him."

"Do you remember what was being said?"

I nod. "She was saying something about him being just as worthless as his father. She called him a lot of names."

"Like what?" he asks me.

I swallow and look at the judge. "I'm… not really sure I can say them in court. The language used was… atrocious," I say quietly.

"Go ahead, Ms. Sharpe," the judge says with an encouraging smile.

"Okay." I take a breath and look at Mr. Anderson. He's the safest place for my eyes right now. "She called him a piece of shit. A motherfucking brat. A stupid cunting asswipe. She said that if he wanted to act like his father, he can go live with him in his rat-infested apartment. She told him that he was a freak just like his father because he fucks men behind her back. She said he probably had sexual partners in front of Layne and turned him gay because he's a sick fuck."

"And during this time, what was Layne doing?"

I shake my head. "Nothing. He was walking away. It wasn't just the language that got me to stop. It was the look on her face. It was almost demonic. She was looking at him with such hate that I could almost feel it emanating from her. But it was when she grabbed his arm and yanked on it that made me start moving towards them. She kept screaming at him. Layne didn't say anything at all except that he was going to be late to school. As soon as those words were out of his mouth, she slapped him so hard, I could both hear it and feel like it was me she'd slapped. I started running towards them as soon as I saw her raise her hand to him, but I didn't get there in time. Her hand connected with his face right before I was able to get there. I pulled Layne away from her."

"Did Layne do anything at all at that time?"

"No, sir. He was actually coming with me. He didn't say anything to her. He had his hand up to his face. It was like he was in shock. I don't think he realized what happened."

"Objection. Speculation," Desiree's attorney says.

I furrow my brows and look at Mr. Anderson. "I don't know what that means," I say quietly.

He gives me a slight shake of his head. "Ms. Sharpe felt like he didn't realize it. We're not in a criminal proceeding here," he says. "She's stating how she felt."

"Overruled," the judge says. Desiree's attorney sits down with a scowl.

"What happened next?" Mr. Anderson asks.

I have no idea what just happened, but I take a deep breath and focus completely on the questions being asked of me. "As I was pushing Layne away from her with the intention of taking him to my house, where he's been numerous times, as that is where his boyfriend lives, Mrs. Rens grabbed my hair and yanked me backwards. I shrieked. Layne pushed her arm away from me. She loosened her grip on me, and I shoved her away from me. She stumbled and fell. As she was stumbling, she slapped me and scratched me. Layne pulled me away, and we took off at a jog towards my house."

"And during this time, what was being said?"

"Mrs. Rens called me a whore. I was accused of sleeping with her husband. Then with her son. As we were running away, she screamed at me that she'd get me. I don't know what she meant."

"And at that time, had you ever seen her before?"

I nod. "I had. It's not the first time I'd seen her hit Layne."

"There was another time?"

I nod again. "It was a couple of months before. I'm sorry. I don't remember exactly the day, but it was during the summer months. I saw her through her window while I was on my walk. She was yelling at him. I couldn't make out what was being said because they were inside, but I could hear that she was yelling at him. She slapped him. I ran home and called the police right away. I had my statement taken and watched the officer speak with her."

"And do you know what came of it?"

I shake my head. "No, sir."

He nods. "Thank you, Ms. Sharpe. I have no further questions."

The other attorney gets up before Mr. Anderson even has a chance to sit down. He strides towards me very intimidatingly. I shrink back and glance at Matt with wide eyes. He gives me a smile and wink. Luca gives me a thumbs up. Layne is smiling. The woman's eyes are shining brightly. And DJ is sitting completely straight. Stoic and unmoving. But when my eyes land on him, I can see the quirk of a smile and the slight nod he gives me. My heart lightens a little, but it's the courage to go on that fills me.

"Ms. Sharpe. What is your relationship with Mr. Rens? And let me remind you that you are under oath."

I knew the question would be coming, but it throws me off anyway because of how aggressive he's asking it. "Um…" My eyes flick to Luca, panicked. He gives me a smile and an encouraging nod, but it doesn't help. For the first time, his gestures don't stop the rising anxiety.

"Are you in a relationship with Mr. Rens or not, Ms. Sharpe? It's a simple question."

"U-um…" I force myself to take a deep breath. My eyes inadvertently flick to DJ. He's watching me. The look on his face is dangerous, but his eyes… They're conveying that it's okay. They're kind and something else. Protective? No. He'd never look at me like that.

"Ms. Sharpe, is this too hard of a question for you?"

"Objection. Badgering," Mr. Anderson says.

"Sustained. Ms. Sharpe?"

I grip the hem of my shirt and glance at her as I take another deep breath. "I… don't have… one. I've never met Mr. Rens."

"But you lived near him for quite a while. Even before he moved out. His best friend is your brother's fiancé. How could you not have met him?"

I shrug and glare at him. "Because I don't like people and typically stay in my room. Whenever Matt or Luca have friends over, I tend to lose myself in work and stay hidden. Layne has become very close to Beckett and is like family to us. It's the only reason I've become comfortable with him."

"So, you don't know Mr. Rens. You hate people. Yet you were outside walking and stepped into a disciplinary action between a mother and her son."

My eyes widen. "She slapped him across the face!"

"Yet, you don't have any idea what it stemmed from, or why it happened. You were just walking by and happened to see it," he says aggressively, like he's mocking me. He rolls his eyes.

I shake my head. "She slapped him across the face and was berating him for everyone to hear! She's not fit to -"

"Not fit to what, Ms. Sharpe?" he growls as he puts his hands on the stand and leans towards me. I fight the urge to flee, but I do push myself further back in the chair.

"Objection, Your Honor! He has no reason to badger and intimidate the witness."

"Sustained. Watch your tone, Mr. Sykes."

"No further questions," the attorney says as he walks back to his table.

I just blink at him before looking in shocked horror at Mr. Anderson. *Did I just do something wrong?* I think to myself. *Did I mess something up and say something I shouldn't have?* I shakily blink a few times to steady my racing heart. I want to scream at him. *How dare he say a slap is just discipline? How dare he justify that as an okay act of parenting? She slapped her son after screaming at him and tearing him down!*

"I have no further questions for this witness, Your Honor," Mr. Anderson says.

"The witness may step down and be seated," the judge says.

I want to disappear. I want to run out of the courtroom and never look back. I don't mean to, but I look at DJ as I stand. I can see so much concern swimming in his eyes as he watches me, but I shake it off because I have to be confused. I'm sure he's grateful that I got up on the stand and said what I said, but there's no way he could be that concerned for someone like me.

I slide into the pew behind DJ. Luca's arm is immediately over my shoulder. He hugs me close. I feel Matt's hand on the back of my neck as he squeezes gently before pulling away. I relax slightly at the reassurance in that gesture.

The woman next to him reaches over and takes my hand. I flinch slightly when it feels like electricity is passing through her hand to mine. My eyes snap to hers in surprise. She's smiling so softly as she squeezes my hand and rubs her thumb over the top of it that I find myself instantly soothed by her.

I smile shyly and slowly pull my hand away as I curl into Luca's side. As soothing as her touch was, it's also terrifying to me that I've had this intense reaction to two people that I've never met before. I came to terms with my sexuality years ago, but I've never actually felt an attraction to anyone the way I do them. It's... overwhelming.

I take a deep shaky breath and force the thoughts from my mind as I focus on Luca's heartbeat in my ear. Now isn't the time for me to analyze this. It can wait. I grip Luca's shirt lightly as I absently pull the collar of my shirt to my nose. I close my eyes and take another shaky breath. I don't know how, but the scent calms me almost instantly.

The touch of her hand...

I can't fathom it, and I'm not sure it makes any sense, but I feel like I've known them both my entire life.

The scent on his shirt...

I have no way to explain how I feel the scent calming me when I have no idea who it belongs to.

Except, I realize with a start, I do know the owner of the scent on this shirt. I stare wide-eyed when his cologne hits my nose as he sits back in his chair.

It belongs to the man sitting right in front of me...

Chapter Seven

✭ DJ ✭

"I'd like to, once again, call Mariah Carter to the stand, please," Mr. Anderson says.

I hear shuffling behind me, but I don't turn around. I've learned very well over the duration of this. Show very little emotion. Showing any at all seems to get me in trouble with Desiree and her attorney.

Mariah makes her way to the stand and gets sworn in. I keep my expression neutral, but inside I'm fucking overjoyed that she's even willing to be up on that stand for me again. This is the third time she's been called to it. And it's the third time she'll have to deal with Desiree's asshole attorney questioning her credibility and relationship status with me.

I growl slightly because I'm still pissed off at how he treated the woman behind me. Lyric. Someone I haven't been able to get off my damn mind since she took out the motherfucker trying to escape from custody a few months ago.

I figured out who she was pretty damn quickly. I know Mariah has had a thing for her for quite a while. They've never exchanged pictures or anything, but Mariah has gone to Matt's with me for football and soccer games. She fell pretty hard for the girl who does her covers. She's always known Lyric's connection to Luca. She's never met her, but she knew who she was.

Not long after we started dating, we sat down and talked about our mutual attraction to Lyric. I know Mariah's sexuality. She's pansexual. I told her about the day at the station and the woman that I saw with Matt. How when one of the assholes tried to escape lockup, she shoved a chair into his path, causing him to lose momentum, allowing for Matt to be able to take him down. I told her that I was in a kind of awe of her because she was clearly scared at the time.

I reassured her that it was more than okay to feel the way she does about Lyric, as I feel the same. I told her that even though I never got to talk to her, I felt a strong connection to her. Ironically, it feels like a completely natural thing. Being in love with each other and attracted to another. Slightly scary, but we've both accepted it.

After we talked, though, we both decided that approaching her in any way about it before the divorce and custody battle has ended just isn't a good idea. Neither of us are in the frame of mind to even consider talking about it with Lyric. We're both pretty wrapped up in ending this so we can all move the hell on. I can't stand seeing the hurt it's causing Layne, and neither can Mariah. We all just want to live our lives without Desiree and her bullshit hanging over us.

"Ms. Carter," Mr. Anderson says. "Please state your full name and spell it for the record."

"Mariah Marie Carter. My first name is M-a-r-i-a-h. The middle is M-a-r-i-e. The last name is C-a-r-t-e-r."

I hear a gasp behind me. I don't need to turn around to see that Lyric, as she had with me a few minutes ago, just figured out who Mariah is and her connection to her. Matt and Luca intentionally didn't tell her because it's better for me if she isn't aware of her connection to any of us. For all anyone knows, she's anonymous to me. And her having no idea who Mariah is also bodes well for me because no one can say that Mariah got Lyric to help me by lying about what happened.

"Thank you, Ms. Carter. You're here today to discuss the events that occurred on the day of September twelfth of this year. Can you describe for us what happened?"

"I can. On September twelfth, I received a phone call from Lieutenant Matthew Chance of the Gainesville Police Department. He said that something had happened with Layne Rens, DJ Rens' son. I asked him what it was. He said that he didn't see it, but Layne told him his mother hit him."

"Objection. Hearsay."

I roll my eyes at Desiree's attorney and shake my head. His objections are getting frivolous and annoying as fuck. I want this to end so badly, I'm almost shaking, but I won't show any of that. I know I need to play the calm one in this shitshow.

"There's nothing that was just said that the police report doesn't already prove. The witness is merely stating what a police officer told her that is verified by the facts in a police report and backed up by evidence," Mr. Anderson says. I crack a small smile because he's really fucking good. I hired him for a reason. "Not only that, but we've already heard Layne's testimony of those events. Ms. Carter is simply corroborating information we already know."

"Overruled," the judge says tiredly. I don't even think she heard anything that was just said.

"Ms. Carter? Please. Continue."

Mariah glances at the other attorney before focusing back on mine. "Lieutenant Chance asked me if I would be willing to take Layne for a little while, as Mr. Rens was in court at the time. Layne was very upset and told me later on, when he did get to my apartment, that he was really upset and would not have been able to focus on classes. He texted Beckett, his boyfriend, and asked him if he could please grab any work he missed for the day."

"Objection! Hearsay!" her attorney says again.

"Overruled," the judge says with a glare.

"When Layne got to your apartment, what did you notice?" Mr. Anderson continues, as if he hadn't been interrupted at all.

"Well, I immediately noticed the black eye. His face was red. His lip was puffy. He told me that his mother only hit him one time, but I asked him a couple of times if he was sure about that. To me, and I'm not an expert, it looked like he'd been hit at least twice. Or once with some heavy object or something. Like a book. He told me both times I asked that it was only once. But it was really hard and made him see stars. He said that he didn't know what exactly happened until his mom was fighting with Ms. Sharpe."

"Ms. Sharpe. The woman who testified before you?"

Mariah nods. "Yes, sir. He told me that his mom started pulling her hair and scratching her. So he pulled Ms. Sharpe away. He told me his mother stumbled and fell, so they ran to Ms. Sharpe's home. Ms. Sharpe called Lieutenant Chance because Layne begged her not to call the police."

"And why is that?"

"Because he didn't want his mother to find a way to use the incident in court against his father."

"Objection, Your Honor. I can't even begin to tell you how much hearsay just came out of her testimony."

"Your Honor, this is all stuff this court has heard already. Ms. Carter is doing nothing but corroborating testimony we've heard from Layne, Lieutenant Chance, Mr. Rens, and Ms. Sharpe."

"Overruled," the judge growls with a glare so vicious that I actually shiver.

"Ms. Carter, please continue," Mr. Anderson says.

Mariah, who is usually very good about ignoring Desiree and her dick attorney, shoots them both a ferocious glare. Keeping my eyes on her, I clear my throat. It's subtle, but it's enough of a command for her eyes to jerk to mine.

I hear a soft, yet sharp, intake of breath behind me from Lyric and something that sounds like a sniffle. Luca's voice is a low rumble of a whisper as he soothes and calms her. I can hear him quietly reassure her that it won't be much longer, and he'll take her home.

I keep my hands folded on the table, but that one sound both pulls at my heartstrings and makes my chest tighten. I want to be the one soothing her and telling her it's all going to be okay. It's completely irrational, considering I really have never met her officially, but it's something I have to push aside and revisit later.

I keep my eyes on Mariah and don't move anything more than my head in an almost imperceptible shake. We don't need her losing control right now. This is way too close to being over, and I know my girl. She might be shy and introverted, but she's fucking savage when she wants to be.

Mariah blinks and takes a breath, a visible sign that not only is she obeying my command; she's bringing herself back from the ledge that fucker put her on. She clears her throat and shifts in the witness chair before folding her hands in her lap. To anyone who can't see her, they'd never know she's digging a fingernail into her palm. It grounds her. She'd never hurt herself, but the pressure helps her to know she's okay; to just breathe.

"Layne did some reading. I kept up with ice for him. I made sure he ate. That afternoon, Mr. Rens got home after finding out what happened when he was done with court for the day. He was upset about what happened. Layne told him exactly what he had me. We all had dinner at Mr. Rens' apartment, which I made. I wanted them both to be able to come down from the day and discuss what happened with no interruptions. When Layne went to his room to study and talk to Beckett, Mr. Rens and I went to my apartment. He wanted to talk and vent about everything without bringing his son into it or risking him overhearing. We both just wanted Layne to have a quiet night."

"And did he?"

Mariah nods. "He did. Mr. Rens made sure of it."

Mr. Anderson nods. "Thank you, Ms. Carter. No further questions."

I give Mariah a soft smile when her eyes meet mine again. She always gets nervous as fuck when Mr. Sykes gets up to ask her questions. It's like all he's trying to do is discredit her and me. I get that's his job, but he's extremely aggressive about it, and I don't like how it makes her feel afterwards. Mariah is a very strong woman, but she has her own demons. Literally. It's hard for her to compartmentalize and not take things personally.

"Ms. Carter, did you take Layne to the hospital?" Mr. Sykes asks.

Mariah blinks a few times. "No. There wasn't a need."

"You said yourself just a few minutes ago that you're not an expert, right?"

"Well, yeah. I'm not a doctor," she says quietly. I have to swallow down my protective growl because I know damn well her demon is making her second guess her actions.

"So, how would you know there wasn't a need?"

She furrows her brows. I keep my eyes trained on her and do everything I can to support her. "I do have emergency training."

"Oh. So, you're an EMT."

"No -"

"A paramedic?"

"No, I'm -"

"No? You're not certified as either of those things. What possible training can you have that would lead you to believe a boy who was supposedly so injured doesn't need to go to the hospital?"

"I have the same amount of training that any police officer does, Mr. Sykes." Her voice drips with venom as she clenches her teeth and glares. There she is. There's my girl.

"So, you're a police officer?"

She shakes her head. "I didn't say that. I said I have the training."

"You're trained as a police officer but aren't one. Have you ever been one?"

"No."

"You've never been one. But you're going to tell me that because you're trained as one, you can make the same decisions as a first responder would. Is that correct?"

Mariah's glare turns as venomous as her voice. Her eyes turn glacier. I just grin and lean back in my chair for the first time during any hearing I've been through since this entire bullshit started. I've been very careful to show no emotion, but I can't help it this time. This fucker is about to wish he never passed the bar exam. And I'm going to sit here and watch without giving her any kind of a signal to cool it this time.

I hear Lyric let out an almost silent whimper behind me.

Huh. Very interesting. That whimper sounded almost like longing. Desire. At the same time, a little fearful. Like she's fighting herself on whether to be attracted to her for showing that protectiveness of both herself and Layne, or be afraid of her for how quickly that switch was flipped. I can't help but wonder what the fuck would bring on a fear like that. Something else I'll have to revisit later, but definitely on my agenda as Mariah and I get to know her.

And we *will* be getting to know her.

"I spoke with a trained officer who didn't believe Layne needed to see a doctor. Lieutenant Chance took him to me instead of the hospital because he believed Layne was fine. Layne was showing no signs of a concussion," Mariah growls as she glares. "He wasn't sick. He wasn't nauseated in any manner. He didn't complain at all about not being able to see or being dizzy or having blurred vision. He was able to move without delay; speak without delay. He could put his head down and play games on his phone, text, and even read a book. He could write. He did all of that without issues."

"But he could have had an issue, right? People all of the sudden have brain aneurysms all the time when they've experienced trauma to the head, right?"

"I can't speak to that. I'm not a doctor."

"But you have enough training to tell us that nothing was wrong with him."

"I never said nothing was wrong with him. I described his injuries. And based on my knowledge, experience, and training, Layne did not need to go to the hospital. I am smart enough to know that if things had changed, then to call emergency services."

"But you admitted that you and Mr. Rens left Layne alone. You went to your apartment where he vented to you about his day."

"Yes. I did."

"Shouldn't that have been during a time that you should have been keeping a close eye on him?"

"Again. From all of my observations, Layne did not need any medical attention that went beyond an ice pack, some Tylenol, and a lot of love."

"What were you and Mr. Rens doing in your apartment?"

"I told you. We were talking."

"Just talking?"

"Yes."

"Objection," Mr. Anderson intercedes. He probably could have long ago, but I think he was enjoying the show as much as I was. I lean forward and clasp my hands together once more. "Council is fishing at a relationship between Mr. Rens and Ms. Carter that we've established over and over again."

"Sustained. Move on, Mr. Sykes."

Mr. Sykes lets out a low growl that makes Mariah shrink back slightly, even though her glare remains. The protective asshole in me rears up. I force myself to stay calm, but I grip my hands a lot tighter.

"You said Lieutenant Chance didn't believe medical attention was required either. Is that correct?"

"Yes," Mariah seethes.

"Is he a doctor?"

"No. He's a -"

"Is he an EMT or Paramedic?"

"No. He's a -"

"He's a police officer with the Gainesville Police Department. He's not a trained medical professional either, and you went on his word that Layne didn't need medical attention after allegedly being slapped so badly, that he had bruises and scratches."

Mr. Anderson lets out a low growl of his own as he starts to stand and object once more. But I put a hand on his arm. I know my girl. She probably has more legal knowledge than the fucker questioning her. And definitely knows far more about what we go through for training as cops than this motherfucker obviously does.

Mariah calmly clears her throat. "Mr. Sykes, it is quite evident to me that you do not know what police officers go through when they are being trained for the field," she hisses through gritted teeth. I grin. "But I do. I know that Lieutenant Chance and every other cop in the entire country receives training as a first responder. In case you aren't aware of the differences between a first responder, EMT, and paramedic over that of someone just getting CPR certification, please allow me to enlighten you."

Mr. Sykes chuckles, obviously having no idea he's about to get fucking schooled. "Go ahead, Ms. Carter. Please. The floor is all yours."

"When you get your CPR certification, you are taught how to use an AED, that is an automated external defibrillator. It's used in the field to shock a person's heart when there is no pulse detected. You are taught to give compressions. One hundred a minute. You are taught that you don't need to give breaths anymore as you used to. That's it. That's all you're taught. A first responder is taught how to give CPR, use a defibrillator, take a blood pressure, use smelling salts, check a person's eyes for signs of a concussion, see signs of traumatic injury, and even patch up wounds. An EMT can do everything a paramedic can do except inserting an IV and inserting a breathing tube. So, when Lieutenant Chance made the decision to take him to me instead of the hospital, I trusted that decision. And, because I have the *exact same training* as he does, he trusted me, as did Mr. Rens and Layne himself, to be able to make a conscious decision on whether or not Layne needed any further medical treatment. Treatment that I would have gotten him had he needed it, Mr. Sykes."

Mr. Sykes sighs and shakes his head. "No further questions."

I chuckle as Mr. Anderson stands. I look up at him questioningly. "I'd like to redirect," he says. The judge nods. "Ms. Carter, you said you had the same training as a police officer. Can you describe what that training was, please? I know you described the medical side, but I'd like to hear the rest."

"Sure. I went through two and half years of school. I got my associate of science degree in Law Enforcement. Part of the training was hands-on courses that included domestic violence response, defensive tactics, and emergency response. We were all certified as first responders with training in CPR and the use of defibrillators. We were trained to recognize head trauma and signs of something worse. We were trained in what to do in those situations. I'm still current in all of my first responder training. I renew it every two years. I was also trained and certified as an EMT. That is not something police officers typically do, but I did it. I'm not anymore, as I let that lapse when I chose not to become a police officer. I still do courses in trauma response, though. Physical, emotional, and mental. And I am certified as a trauma responder."

"And do you have a job where that certification is used?"

"Sort of. I don't get paid for it, but Lieutenant Chance does CIT training, or critical incident training, with all of the officers at the department. I go in and do real life scenarios for the officers to respond to. Some of them are domestic violence related. I assist in training police officers how to not only spot signs of physical trauma, but mental and emotional as well."

"And with all of that training and experience, in your opinion, was Layne Rens in need of any further medical attention than what he had already received previously from EMT and Paramedics who were at Lieutenant Chance's house earlier that day, per his earlier testimony?"

"No. I do not believe he did."

"And did he at any other time over the past three months since the day of the incident?"

"No. He has not. He has been to his doctor for a regularly scheduled medical check-up. Mr. Rens did ask him how things were looking and if he seemed healthy and happy. The doctor told us both, as I was there with them, that Layne is a very healthy boy."

"Why were you there with them that day, Ms. Carter?" Mr. Anderson turns and winks at me. I grin because I know exactly what he's doing. When he's done, there will be no question about what type of father I am.

"I was asked to go by Mr. Rens because he didn't want any doubt in anyone's mind that he is a good father and does everything he needs to do for his son. I also go grocery shopping with them, mostly online since I don't do well around people. As you and the court know, I have anxiety and panic disorders and do not do well around large crowds. Mr. Rens makes sure that all of Layne's needs are fully met and makes sure that he has witnesses to corroborate that."

Mr. Anderson nods and looks up at the judge. "As we've already established today, Ms. Carter is not the only one who has witnessed my client being a good father to his son." He nods to Mariah. "I have no further questions for you, Ms. Carter. Thank you for your time."

"You may step down, Ms. Carter. Thank you," the judge says. I give her a subtle wink as she hurries back to her seat. She lets out a breath. Matt quietly reassures her. The judge takes a deep breath. "Over the course of the past year, I have seen a lot of things come across my bench regarding this case. In the interest of fairness, I'll be looking over everything. We'll reconvene today after lunch at…" She looks at her watch. "At one-thirty." She stands and bangs her gavel. "Dismissed until then."

"All rise!" the bailiff barks. We all do as we're told. When the judge disappears into her chambers, Desiree and her attorney quickly hurry for the door. Her entourage follows her, all of whom were on the stand for her this morning.

I glance at my watch. "Eleven-thirty. We have two hours."

"This will end today. The judge has had enough of her antics. It was pretty obvious today. Frankly, I don't think she has anything else up her sleeve," Mr. Anderson says. "Go have lunch with your family. Leave the courthouse. Just breathe and come down from everything we've gone through this morning."

"What if she tries to say something about her legal case that's pending?" a sweet, quiet voice says. My breath catches, and I chance looking at Lyric.

"She tried this morning, baby. It didn't work," I answer, my voice a little raspy.

Her eyes widen as she nods slowly. I intentionally called her 'baby' to see how she'd react. I expected the surprise. I didn't expect the sexy blush and the tongue that darted out quickly to lick her lower lip, nor her slight lowering of her eyes. My mind shoots back to Matt mentioning Lyric is a natural submissive.

Fuck.

My dick is suddenly at full attention. I quickly grab the folder I have with a stack of papers in it and hold it in front of myself.

I also didn't expect the quiet moan to escape Mariah's throat that's probably imperceptible to anyone but me, since I'm standing so close to her. Matt lets out a low chuckle and gives me a knowing smirk. Luca shoots me a glare and pulls Lyric closer to him. Protectively. He knows I'm with Mariah. I have no doubt that I'll be facing a conversation with Lyric's brother in the near future.

Between Mariah's and Lyric's beautiful sounds and looks, I know I'm not going to survive much longer without both of them. Like Mariah, I feel like a piece of us is missing. We have each other. We have Layne.

We just need Lyric.

This shit needs to end.

Today.

Chapter Eight

☆ Mariah ☆

I nervously cross my legs as my foot bounces while we wait for the judge to announce what's going to happen. We all feel like we know what she'll say, but until those words come out of her mouth, we just don't know what she's going to do.

The judge clears her throat. Matt rests his hand palm up on my thigh. I take it gratefully. I need the support right now. I don't dare reach for DJ and don't want to scare Lyric. I'm pretty sure when I gave into my need to touch her, it scared the crap out of her. She pulled away slowly, but I saw the confusion and fear in her eyes. I hated it.

"After going through all of this, I need to apologize," the judge begins. I furrow my brows. "I have, unfortunately, seen people go to great lengths to get what they want in my courtroom. And I do have to entertain any new evidence that comes across my desk."

My heart sinks. I look at Matt. Instant tears fill my eyes. He squeezes my hand in reassurance, but I can see the vein in his neck ticking as he glares at the judge. I take a shaky breath and look back at her. I can tell DJ has tensed because the muscles in his back are coiled. I think if this goes on any longer, DJ might actually snap.

"The apology stems from all of those extra hearings we had to schedule in order to get through this all. Now, Mrs. Rens, you've asked the court for alimony, child support, and full custody of Layne Rens, your fourteen-year-old son." The judge looks up from the papers in front of her. "You've attempted to prove on multiple occasions that Mr. Rens was cheating on you, but you've presented no evidence to me. Nothing but your word. You've stated that Mr. Rens was abusive to both you and the son you both share, but you've given me nothing but police reports that all state the opposite of what you've told me and what the officers who Mr. Rens and his attorney have asked to testify. Mr. Rens was never once taken into custody for any of the alleged incidents. You and your son never presented with any injuries that would prove your allegations. I have not seen any images of injuries you have alleged you had. I want to reiterate that nothing you've given this court, including your witness' testimony, has proven your allegations against Mr. Rens."

I can't help the smirk of satisfaction that crosses my face. I glance at Desiree. Her head is down. She's slumped in her chair, and I know I heard her sniffle. Her parents and sister are all glaring at the judge and her attorney.

"Mr. Rens," the judge looks at DJ. "You've proven over and over that Mrs. Rens cheated on you not only once, but several times. Your witness' testimony corroborated everything you've stated and they've even defended you on several occasions." She looks down at the papers once more before looking back up. A sense of hopefulness fills me. Maybe this really will end today. "I see you've offered several settlements that have all been rejected by her. This last one gives her the house, her vehicle, a substantial cash settlement and fifty percent custody of your son. That was turned down by Mrs. Rens and her attorney. Since then, you've offered nothing and allowed it to come here, to my courtroom. Just today, your attorney has given me your final offer."

That little flicker of hope sits in my chest but dims when I hear DJ inhale a shaky breath.

"Mrs. Rens, in the State of Florida, upon divorce with no prenuptial agreement, you would be entitled to half of all of Mr. Rens' assets, including alimony. Because there is overwhelming evidence, including both video and audio recordings above and beyond the testimony of several people involved with you, you aren't entitled to anything.

However, Mr. Rens has still generously offered to allow you to keep your vehicle, though it belongs to him, as you are not named on the title, the home, which also belongs to him, as you are not named on the deed. He's also offered to continue to pay the property taxes on the home for you. He's requested full custody in the matter of Layne Rens."

I squeeze Matt's hand harder. I can hear Lyric breathing a little faster, though I'm not sure how, considering my own heart is racing at a deafening speed.

"I am going to honor Mr. Rens' newest offer with exceptions. Mrs. Rens, the house belongs to you. Mr. Rens specifically states that he doesn't want it because of all that happened. Too many bad memories. He doesn't want the money from selling it. He doesn't want the house or anything in it. I am granting that request. I have the deed. Mr. Rens will sign it over before he leaves the courtroom today. My exception is that the property taxes are not his responsibility once the house becomes yours. The house is paid off. It becomes yours free and clear. The property taxes and anything else in the house, including maintenance, are your responsibility. The vehicle is yours, as Mr. Rens has also stated he doesn't want it or have use for it. He doesn't want the money from selling it. He wants nothing. Mr. Rens has paid it off in full. I have the title. It will be signed over to you today. These are two very generous gifts you're being given because you aren't at all entitled to either of them under Florida law."

DJ exhales. I feel him relax slightly, but he won't relax completely until the matter of Layne and the custody is taken care of. None of us will.

"Now, in the matter of Layne Rens. We know that the DNA test that was requested by Mr. Rens' attorney came back that he is Layne's biological father, despite Mrs. Rens stating that she didn't believe he was. Usually, I don't grant one parent full custody. Not unless there are circumstances that overwhelmingly tell me that one parent is unfit. In this case, that's what happened." She pauses as if she's trying to compose herself.

I know the feeling. I glance at Beckett and Layne. Beckett is sitting next to Layne holding his hand. Lyric is on the other side of Layne. Luca is at the end of the row. Lyric keeps glancing at Layne and wringing her hands.

"I know there are worse cases in the world, but I've never been a part of one. I've never been sickened by the testimony of a child, or horrified by the images I saw of injuries he sustained three months ago. Like I previously stated, I know there are far worse cases of child abuse in this world, but never has one come to me. I've been lucky in not having to deal with a single one. Usually, the circumstances come down to finances. Nothing like this. Alcohol and drug use. Sexual encounters with multiple men. All while he is in the home."

DJ's shoulders slump a little bit at the judge's words. My heart breaks for him. I can hear Lyric sniffle quietly. I glance at her and notice that she's just as in tune to him as I am and noticed the change in his posture as well. I watch her bite her lip and wipe her eyes. Her compassion for him makes the feelings I have stirring for her even more intense. Heated.

The judge takes a breath. "Mrs. Rens, I am not granting you any custody. None. For three reasons. The first is because of the abuse. All of it. Physical, mental, and emotional. The drug and alcohol use. The sexual encounters. It's all abuse to that child. The second is because of the several people, including your own family, who stated that you never wanted children. The several witnesses who testified up here who stated that not only did you never want them, the only reason you're asking for full custody of Layne is because of the money. Those are words they heard you say. Furthermore, you were caught on audio and video on one of the sex tapes that was entered into evidence saying that exact same thing. I will not allow that child to suffer like that."

Out of the corner of my eye, I see Luca take Lyric's shaking hands in his. Beckett is soothingly running his thumb over the back of Layne's hand. Layne is sitting almost as stoically as DJ is. But I can see his eyes are wet. Matt, though he's trying to be strong for me, squeezes my hand a little tighter. It's the only sign he's given that he's as upset about hearing all of this as we all are.

"The third is because Layne is old enough to make his own decisions when it comes to his custody. He's clearly stated on more occasions than should be necessary that he wants nothing at all to do with his mother and prefers to live with his father. Layne has told the court that his father takes care of him, loves him, provides for him, and supports him. He's stated he doesn't feel safe with you. He's stated he feels you're unstable. He's stated he fears your actions when you're doing drugs and drinking alcohol. His testimony was backed up by police reports where your blood alcohol level was three times the legal limit, and by audio and video where you're drinking and doing drugs. So, when it comes to the matter of the custody of Layne Rens, I award full custody to Mr. Rens, Layne's father. That is my judgment."

She bangs her gavel, but stays seated as both DJ's and Desiree's attorney's approach the bench. DJ's tough guy composure finally breaks. His head falls to the desk, and his shoulders lift and fall. There's no mistaking that even though he's not making a sound, he's crying silent tears of relief and happiness.

Matt reaches forward, still holding my hand, and rubs his hand up and down DJ's back. He squeezes his shoulder. DJ takes a deep breath and stands. He turns just as Layne stands. They both throw their arms around each other and hug each other long and hard as they sway back and forth. We all could join, but we don't. None of us are about to interrupt a moment like this between a father and his son.

★★★

DJ parks his car in Matt's driveway and loosens his tie. He grins when Layne jumps out of the backseat and runs inside the house.

"He's been away from Beckett for fifteen minutes." DJ laughs as he puts his tie in the cup holder and undoes the top three buttons of his shirt.

"Well, more like twenty." I smile as we both get out of the car. I start heading to the house.

DJ takes my hand and pulls me against him. "Hey." He wraps his arms around me as I look up at him. "Thank you. For everything. You were great up there."

I melt against him and rest my head against his chest. He sways gently with me and kisses the top of my head. "I tried."

"You did incredible. I'm proud of you. I know it wasn't easy."

"No…, but… it's over."

DJ squeezes me a little tighter and kisses my head again. "I'm proud of you."

"Hey! Jackass!" Matt says from behind me. "Get your ass in here. We need to talk."

I furrow my brows and glance over my shoulder at Matt. He's leaning against the side of his house with his arms folded over his chest. His tie is undone and hanging over his shoulders and down his chest. Like DJ, the top three buttons on his shirt are undone. I have to chuckle because while DJ is wearing nice suit pants, Matt is wearing blue jeans. Yet he still looks just as professional.

"Here we go," DJ rumbles. I glance up when I see curtains moving out of the corner of my eye. DJ follows my gaze. In an upstairs bedroom, Lyric is standing near a window that's half open. Her arms are wrapped around herself. "God, she's beautiful," DJ whispers.

"I know. Breathtaking." I shiver. I'm not sure if she hears us, but she darts from her window almost as quickly as she appeared.

Matt chuckles as DJ takes my hand and leads me into the house. "I know that you two will be everything she needs and all she never realized she wants. But Luca is on a fucking warpath."

DJ chuckles. "Just with me, though, huh?"

Matt laughs. "He likes Mariah a lot better than you. She's nicer. And prettier."

I giggle. "But… Luca doesn't swing my way."

Matt grins. "Neither do I. And I still think you're prettier." He hugs me when we reach him and follows us back inside.

As soon as we cross the threshold, the amount of people here is slightly overwhelming, but that isn't what strikes me. It's the intense glare coming from across the room. Lyric's brother is obviously more protective than she ever mentioned to me in our chats, if I can conclude that from the way he's staring DJ down.

DJ lets out a low sigh of defeat and follows Matt towards Luca. I look outside and decide against going out there right now. There aren't that many people, but while I know who they are, I don't really associate with them. So instead, I make my way to the kitchen. If I know anything at all about Matt and Luca, and I do, I know they're terrible about putting finished dishes in serving bowls. I intentionally bought them two sets of serving bowls because it annoyed me. If they insist on being social butterflies and having people over, the least they can do is serve things on platters that look good. Not like the ones they ordered out of a Tupperware catalog.

I blink when my hunch is completely wrong. Impressively, there are a lot of baked goods all neatly placed on trays and covered. They are spread across the counter. The refrigerator is full of things in serving bowls or on serving trays. Knowing that Matt and Luca are horrendous bakers, even though they're amazing cooks, I have to wonder if the baked deliciousness is the work of Lyric.

I'm pretty sure that all of this organization and perfection is her. The realization that she had all of this ready because, even with how nervous she was, she was hopeful that everything would turn out okay; that Layne would be safe with his dad, makes my already deep feelings for her intensify. I know when DJ discovers all of this, he'll feel the same way I do. It makes my heart fill with even more love and adoration for her.

The laughter coming from outside makes me smile. I'm really happy that some of DJ's closest friends came to support him and congratulate him. I know that Matt and Luca have had this set up for a long time, but each postponement of a judgment meant pushing this celebration back. The fact that everyone that was invited is here makes me happy because it means showing DJ and Layne support that they need. I wonder if that means Lyric's baked desserts went to waste those other times. I have a feeling she probably cooked them all those times as well.

I busy myself making the watermelon punch DJ asked for, but my eyes snap up to a quiet whimper and whisper. Layne and Beckett are each holding one of Lyric's hands and speaking quietly to her. I can't hear the conversation, but my eyes are drawn to the beautiful woman who has been seared into my mind for such a long time.

Putting a face to the name is an incredible feeling because it means I don't have to imagine her anymore. Though, Lyric in real life is nothing like the woman in my dreams. She far surpasses any fantasy I've conjured up. She not only leaves me breathless, but speechless as well.

Which is why I don't say a word to her when Layne and Beckett tug her into the kitchen. It's not because I don't want to. It's because I'm a little afraid I'll make a fool of myself. Or that I'll scare her like I did when I took her hand after her testimony. That's the last thing I want.

Instead, I smile softly at her and wish for DJ. He's so good at talking to people and making them feel at ease. I wish I had those skills. When I'm around people, I just want to dart under a table or into a dark room and burrow into myself. I fight it. I'm not to the point where I refuse to come out of my house for anything, but the reasons I leave are few and far between. And I will only go to a place I feel safe.

Like here.

"This… is Mariah," Beckett says with a huge smile. "*The* Mariah. The one you really like."

Lyric's eyes widen. She squeaks adorably as she blushes and swats Beckett's arm. "Would you stop that?" she whisper hisses. Almost like she doesn't think I hear her.

Layne grins widely. "Nope!"

She pushes him lightly. "Brat. Why do I tolerate you?"

"Because you love us!" they both say at the same time right before they kiss her cheek. Layne winks at me as he tugs Beckett out of the kitchen with him. I shoot him a glare that makes him laugh.

"I'm stealing your Playstation for that, trouble!" she calls after them. "Ugh. They're both brats. Insufferable."

"They really are," I say softly as I shake my head. "They once forced me out of my cocoon in ninety degree weather just because they wanted me to meet this girl that they were mildly infatuated with." I shake my head. "And not even like the 'I have a crush on you' way. The 'you're so interesting and smart that I want to work with you on all things ever' way."

Lyric giggles. "You must be talking about Lyla. They do everything with her."

I nod with a smile. "That was her name! My apartment complex has a private pool. They were hanging out with me because DJ was going to be late getting home. Lyla changed over at DJ's house and headed straight for the pool. They dragged me out, nearly kicking and screaming, literally, because it was so nice out and they wanted to swim. But DJ has a rule. Since it's still technically a public pool, even though it's just for residents, he wants them to have a chaperone. Just to make sure nothing happens."

Lyric smiles softly as she starts removing wrappings on the baked goods. "He sounds like a really great guy and an amazing father," she says quietly.

I nod. "He is."

"I'm sorry I never came out of my room to meet you or him." The words are barely above a whisper, but I can just make them out. I hate the regret and self recrimination I hear.

I let out a breath as I turn towards the refrigerator. "You really shouldn't think that way about yourself," I say quietly, but firmly. "You're so much better than how you view yourself." It's a hard lesson to learn but an important one. One DJ is working on with me every single day. One I have been working on with Lyric over our chats.

"Yes, ma'am…," Lyric whispers. And I don't know why those words stir something deep within me and makes me a little wet. Who am I kidding? A lot. A lot wet. It's the same as it is reading the words on a screen.

I don't have any idea how to tell her everything I want to. Like how pretty she is. How much I like her. How I've imagined her in a lot of different positions while I have my way with her. I'm not good at any of this. The images all of my thoughts conjure makes me blush.

Furiously.

I close my eyes for a moment before pulling out one of the dishes. I smile as I turn, choking down my own thoughts. "So, I finally get to put a face to the woman I've been slowly falling in love with." It's not what I intended to say, but it's what feels right.

She lets out a quiet squeak as her eyes shoot to mine. "Wh-what?"

Her British accent is adorable, but I think I really like it a lot when she stammers. It's so cute, and she looks so pretty when she's flustered.

Before I get a chance to respond, though, DJ walks out of the room that Matt and Luca dragged him to. Luca looks a little more at ease. Matt is beaming. DJ's eyes meet mine, and he gives me a megawatt grin. Out of the corner of my eye, I notice Lyric's eyes are on his as well. I realize all at once that I'm not the only one DJ is looking at, and I couldn't be happier to see it.

"DJ! We've been waiting forever, man! Come out here! We got you a beer!" someone yells from outside. Lyric jumps and instantly looks down, like she was caught doing something she shouldn't be.

"In a minute," DJ rumbles, without breaking his stride nor taking his eyes off us.

"You know," I say quietly, but loud enough for the approaching DJ to hear. I lean a little closer to her. "It's okay to be attracted to him. He's rather irresistible, isn't he?"

DJ chuckles as he reaches us. "Not as irresistible as you are, sweetheart." He leans down and kisses me softly before straightening and turning to Lyric. He reaches up and curls a lock of her hair around his finger.

She gasps almost silently and looks between us wide-eyed. "It's no-"

"Just as she said. It's okay for you to be attracted to me, It's just as okay for you to be attracted to Mariah," he continues with a grin, cutting her off gently.

She squeaks quietly, her gaze flitting between us as her breathing picks up. "Y-you don-"

"Just like we both are intensely attracted to you." DJ cuts her off once more and emphasizes his statement with a gentle tug on the lock of hair he holds.

"Y-y-yes, sir," she whispers, but she's trembling. Her eyes still dart between the two of us.

"Take a -" I begin, but Lyric lets out a terrified, though quiet, noise as a few people come in from outside.

"DJ! Come on, man!" one of them says. I don't really see who because my attention is on the fleeing woman who is running up the stairs right now.

I exchange a look with DJ as he growls under his breath, shooting a glare at the loudmouth who scared our girl. We both start after her. Luca, seeing her flee, shoots DJ and I a look and starts after her, but Matt stops him.

"Don't," Matt says quietly, but comfortingly to Luca.

Luca quits pushing against him to get to his sister, but his eyes meet ours in a hard glare. "Don't fuck this up," he growls warningly. "She's been hurt enough."

DJ takes my hand as we walk past them both. "I already told you I'd never fucking do that," DJ responds. I question what they talked about, or what hurt Lyric in the past, but I say nothing. I know DJ will tell me later. It's not important right now anyway.

Lyric is.

He leads me up the stairs, taking them two at a time, effectively making me have to run to keep up with him. When we reach the only closed door on this floor, DJ stops. I squeeze his hand a little tighter as he takes a deep breath.

My heart breaks when I hear her quietly crying and berating herself. I sniffle because her words cut my soul. Like each and every one of them is a knife piercing my skin. I look up at DJ as he quietly knocks on the door. She immediately quiets, but I can still hear her sniffling. I can feel her pain.

"Go back to the celebration, Luca... I'm fine...," her voice comes through the door in a whisper, but I hear the hitch in her breath.

I already know she's not going to answer the door. So does DJ. Usually, we both would respect the privacy of anyone who needs time to themselves, but our future is on the other side of this door, and neither of us are too keen on the way she was talking to herself.

He lets out a breath to steady himself as he reaches for the handle and slowly opens the door...

Chapter Nine

☆ Lyric ☆

"You're so stupid. Of course they noticed you looking. You should have never been looking in the first place. They're together. They would never be interested in you. You're so far beneath them it's laughable…" I pace across the length of my room. I close my eyes and take a deep breath trying to keep from breaking down.

I slowly open my eyes and sit down on the edge of my bed. I wrap my favorite fleece around my shoulders and try to push away the demon battering my mind. I know she's evil and makes me totally irrational.

I growl at myself and shoot to my feet as I start to pace again. It doesn't matter how intense my attraction to Mariah and DJ is. It's inappropriate. It's ridiculous. I've never met either of them before today. Talking online doesn't count.

It's stupid anyway. They're together. There's no place for me there. I won't come between them. I won't wreck a relationship. I may be many things, but that is one thing I have never, nor will I ever be.

"You're delusional. There's no way they meant what they were saying down there. You're not good enough. Not pretty enough. Not sexy en-," I jump and cut myself off at a knock on my bedroom door.

Luca.

I quickly swipe my hands against my eyes and move silently to the door, but I take a few moments to calm my shaky voice. "Go back to the celebration, Luca... I'm fine...," I call out softly, just loud enough for him to hear me.

I swallow hard and close my eyes as I silently beg for him to go back downstairs. I can't handle talking to him right now. I know he'll help me fight her. The demon. My brother always has. But I just can't handle that talk right now.

I turn away from the door and move to stand by my window just out of sight of anyone who might be entering or leaving the house.

You just couldn't help yourself could you? Had to want the two people that you could never have. They would never want you. What could you possibly have to offer them? Other than your body. And even then, no one ever wants you after.

"Lyric...?" a low voice asks. The dominance I hear in it sends shivers straight to my core. I shake my head. I must be imagining it. No way would he be in here. He's downstairs with his beautiful girlfriend; his amazing son. He's surrounded with the love and support of his friends.

I push the palm of my hands against my closed eyes to try and stop the tears from falling as I sob silently. I'm losing the battle against her. I can feel my mind trying to pull me back into that dark pit. I try to forcefully push the thoughts away as hard as I can. I can't go back there. I won't survive this time.

I'm so busy fighting my tears and *her* that I don't hear the door open. Nor do I hear the footsteps moving quickly towards me. Not until I feel a pair of strong arms tugging me into an equally firm chest. I squeak and jump looking up at DJ wide-eyed. His arms lock around me so tightly that I have no choice but to sink against him.

I feel him lead me to my bed and sit down. He tugs me into his lap. I feel another set of arms embrace me. My senses are suddenly overpowered by DJ's masculine and earthy scent and Mariah's soothingly coconut scent. They both hug me so tightly that I feel waves and waves of something I've never felt before washing over me. It feels so different from when Luca and Matt have hugged me after one of my anxiety attacks. I don't know what it is. I'm sure there's not a name for it.

I close my eyes and sink further into their embrace when I feel fingers running through my hair. I don't know if it makes me crazy or not, but I feel so safe and secure here in their arms. Like it's where I belong.

"Shh, baby. We've got you," DJ rumbles in my ear. I feel his lips pressed against my head. Mariah's hand is rubbing my back. I know it's hers, it feels smaller than DJ's hand.

I slowly melt into them and clutch at his waistband without thinking. I squeak and try to pull away when my hand brushes against his cock. Which is hard and very large.

"Shh… It's okay, baby. You're okay," he pulls me back into his chest with a chuckle. "You didn't do anything wrong."

"I-I s-shouldn't h-have…," I trail off with a sniffle not knowing what to say. My eyes widen when I realize I'm in his lap. "S-sor-ry!" I try to scramble up, only for him to grip me tighter.

"Baby, stop," he says with a warning rumble that's so dominant I stop in my tracks because I can do nothing else. "You didn't and aren't doing anything wrong, Lyric," he whispers.

Mariah's lips meet the sensitive flesh of my neck, and I shiver. "You aren't. I'm not upset. You need this, baby."

I shiver again at the pet name and peek back at her. She's smiling softly at me. There's a look in her eye that I can't name, but it fills me with warmth. "I don't u-understand. Why are you here? You're together. You have no need to be here... with me," I say quietly and look down at my hands.

I play with my fingers as I wait for the inevitable. For them to leave. It's like my demon said. I have no place with either of them. She may try to fill me with doubt about myself and my abilities often, but there are a lot of things she's right about. This is one of them.

"We're attracted to you, honey," DJ keeps whispering. His voice is calm and soothing. Just as Mariah's touch. My eyes are so wide right now, I'm not sure they can get any larger. My gaze snaps up to his in shock. "Mariah has been for a long time. Online. It doesn't matter. She fell in love with who you are as a person. I've heard things about you for a long time from Matt and Luca. Even from Layne on occasion. I didn't want to admit it, but I started to fall for you, too. Long ago."

"When he first saw you at the police station when you helped them take down that guy, he couldn't stop thinking about you. We talked about it then. We figured out who you are."

"Nice takedown, by the way," DJ says with a grin.

I blush and duck my head when I remember that day. I was both terrified and elated to have been able to help. I take a deep breath and sniffle. "Then... why... didn't you say anything?" I ask hesitantly, looking back up at them both when I feel DJ's hand tilting my chin up. "A-and... y-you're... t-together...," I trail off and look between them.

A large part of me is squealing in happiness on the inside that they're as attracted to me as I am to them. But the rest of me... is baffled and unsure. *How would that work? Would I be dating them both? Is that even possible?* I shake my head to rid the thoughts and focus back on them.

"Why would you want me, too?" *What on earth could I possibly have to offer you?* is the question I leave unspoken.

"Honestly, we didn't say anything because of the hearing and the case against Desiree," DJ says. "I didn't want to give her any ammunition. If you continued believing that you didn't have a relationship with me, you wouldn't have to be put into a position like Mariah was today. We knew the attorney would try and establish that we've always been more than friends. That I cheated on Desiree. I didn't. I would never do that. We've been separated for over a year. Mariah and I were never anything more than friends until a few months ago. Actually, the night I saw you," he pauses and runs his thumb over my lower lip.

There's a look in his eye that makes me release it from the grip I didn't even know I had on it with my teeth immediately. The dominance in that one look makes me shiver, and my panties soak. Fuck. I've never seen anything sexier than that look in his eye. No one except Mariah has ever had this intense of a reaction from me.

"Sorry, sir," I whisper.

"Good girl." His eyes darken as he continues.

I shiver and bite back a whimper. Part of me wants to drop to my knees in front of him right now. The other, more cynical part, thinks this is too good to be true. *Fuck. Please let it be real.*

"We knew the attorney would try to establish doubt in the judge's head that I had cheated on Desiree first and led her to cheat on me. That was always their plan. That's what they tried to do numerous times through the hearings. But that roadblock is no longer an issue. The hearing today was the end of all her drama. We're free to live our lives as we want to without any worry or stress."

Mariah tugs at the ends of my hair. "We are together," she says softly. "And maybe it's crazy…, but we feel like something is missing."

I tilt my head curiously. "Wh-what?" I hiccup.

"You. You're missing," DJ whispers. He squeezes my hip. "We feel very intensely for you. Just like we do with each other. Does it make sense?" He shakes his head with a grin as he gives me another squeeze. "Nope. But it's not unusual for it to happen. Most people, love strikes once, if they're lucky, and that's all. For us, it struck twice."

"The truth is," Mariah begins. She leans her head on my back as she hugs me. "We have no idea how this will work. What we do know, though, is how we feel about you. And we're pretty sure you feel something for us. As for everyone else and their feelings?" I feel her shrug.

"Fuck them," DJ says. "They don't matter. We do. The three of us. That is, if you want to be with us. It's totally understandable if you tell us to fuck off."

"H-how would that even work…? W-would I be with you, then with Mariah? Would we go on dates individually, one at a time, or all of us together…?" I force myself to pull away from their embrace and stand. I start to pace the room.

"Lyric," DJ rumbles in warning.

But I keep going, unable to stop. "This is insane… There's no way in Hell that you're interested in me… Just look at you, and then at me… You're beautiful and handsome. Smart and witty. Talented and sassy. Protective, possessive, and all the other good words in the dictionary!" I flail my hands and tug on my hair.

"Lyric," Mariah says quietly.

That's right. You'll never be good enough for them. They're fooling you. You're fooling yourself if you think for a second any of this is real. I wipe my eyes furiously and shove *her* away. I can't listen to her.

"I'm none of those things! I have nothing to offer either of you! I'm… nowhere near either of your leagues! I'm clumsy… I'm stupid… I live with my brother because I'm not able to be on my own! That should show you what a freak I am! I'm naive… I'm ugly… I'm broken… I'm fat, for fuck sake! There's no possible way you could be interested in me." I'm rambling, more to myself than to them at this point, as I pace.

"Lyric!" DJ says as he grabs my arm.

I squeak with wide eyes as he spins me around. He has me over his knee before I have a second to even breathe. "I -"

"Nothing that came out of your mouth is okay. Not for a fucking second. And I won't allow it." DJ's hand comes down hard on my ass.

I scream into Mariah's thigh as she tangles her fingers in my hair and whimpers. "Ah!"

"You're *all* of those words you described us as. All of them. You're beautiful. You're fucking smart as hell, strong, witty, talented as fuck, and for Christ sake, fat? You fucking call yourself fat?" DJ slaps my ass again. I feel Mariah jump and grip my hair a little tighter.

"Ah!" I scream again.

"What the hell could possibly make you feel like you're fat? Fuck, Lyric. You're not!" He slaps my ass again. Mariah jumps and whimpers. DJ's hand rests on the globe of my ass. I feel him lean towards her. "Mariah. It's okay. Go get us something to drink, baby."

Mariah sniffles. "Okay…" I feel her shakily get up and hug herself as she hurries to the door. She quickly slips out and closes it behind her.

"I'm sorry…," I whimper. "I d-didn't mean t-to make her l-leave."

"Stop. Stop it, Lyric. She's having a hard time watching someone she's got strong feelings for take a punishment after berating herself like you just fucking did." He slaps my ass again.

"A-ah!" I wriggle as the tears I was trying to stop fall even harder. I hate that I made her sad. I never want to hurt either of them or make them sad.

"I do not *ever* want to hear the words you just uttered out of your mouth again, Lyric," He rumbles dominantly as he squeezes my ass. I shiver at his tone. "You have curves a woman would kill for and a man would fall all over himself to hold. You're so sexy, you have two people, a man and a woman, who want you more than they could ever express. You're so fucking beautiful that Mariah told me you intimidate her. That she didn't think you'd feel like she was good enough for you. She asked me what would happen if you didn't want her. If it would ruin us. And I didn't know how to answer her, baby, because I couldn't for a second see it happening. And I still don't know how to answer that question because neither of us can envision our future without you in it."

I whimper and bury my face in his thigh. I hate the thought that she's been hurting. I hate that it's also been hurting him. I just want to make it better. I feel an ember of hope flickering to life in my chest.

I want that.

I want it all.

His words seep into me slowly, somehow easing me more and more. "I do want her. How could she think I don't?"

"How could you think we don't?" He rubs my butt, soothing the sting away through my jeans. I sniffle and grip his thigh as he continues. "You're taking one more for that rant. The things that came out of your mouth, Lyric, are so beyond the realm of acceptance that I don't even know where to really start. But it never happens again, baby. Never."

"Yes, sir," I whisper with a sniffle. I wipe my eyes as a sense of… calm flows through me. The embers in my chest become a roaring flame. I feel my muscles relax against him. I take a deep breath and grip his thigh, bracing myself. "I can do this. I can be a good girl."

"You are a good girl, baby. A very good girl." His hand comes down on my ass one last time. Hard. Just as hard as the other times. Only this time, I can feel where it's coming from.

Somewhere I've never really felt before.

A place of love.

Could it really be?

DJ gently pulls me up and settles me on his lap once more. With the pad of his thumb, he wipes my tears away. He runs his hand through my hair and tangles it around his fist. Without saying a word, he leans in and kisses me. I let out a soft moan and melt into him, gripping his shoulders lightly.

Fireworks explode in my head. Or maybe it's me. Maybe I'm the firework. Because as soon as his tongue swipes across my lips and touches my tongue when I open for him, inviting him in, my entire body shoots into the air.

He pulls away slowly but keeps me close to him. "There's nothing in this world that should ever make you think so down on yourself or that you aren't worthy of love, baby. I want to hear all of it. Every place that those thoughts came from. But right now…" He kisses me softly again and again for a long moment until Mariah quietly comes back into the room with drinks for all of us. "Right now, it's pretty obvious that you need to know we're serious. Luca said the way to do that..." He tucks a strand of hair behind my ear. I squeak a little at Luca's name. "Is through touch. Actions. They speak louder than words."

Mariah, after setting the drinks down gently guides me off DJ's lap and settles me between the two of them. I watch her curiously. DJ keeps one arm around me as he shifts so he's looking at me. Mariah wraps one arm around me, too, and shifts so she's also looking at me. I look between the two of them curiously.

"There's really only one way I can think of to show you how much we want you while trying to settle your nerves about us both wanting you," she says softly. She reaches up and cups my cheek gently. She leans in and kisses me.

Like the kiss with DJ, I feel like I'm a rocket just taking off into outer space. The outer edges of outer space. Her lips are soft. Far less commanding than DJ's but still everything I've ever needed, and so much more. And just like the kiss with DJ, I let out a soft moan and melt into her. Her fingers find their way down my neck and to my collarbone.

And then I feel DJ's lips against my neck. He keeps one hand firmly on my hip and drops the other to my thigh. If he moved up just an inch, he'd be touching my pussy. My *bare* pussy. I hate underwear. And I hate hair. It makes me itch. Oh God, how I want him to touch me. If Mariah would just move her hand down slightly, she'd be gripping my aching tits. I arch a little as she kisses me, hoping she'll take the hint and give me what I want.

I moan and whimper when she lightly brushes my nipple on her way down my stomach. She kisses down my jaw as DJ kisses up to my lips. He slides his tongue into my mouth and flicks it over mine. I close my eyes and grip both of their thighs.

Mariah slides her hand across my stomach and back up to my other breast as she licks then sucks my neck. I gasp again and moan when she squeezes lightly before doing the same thing to the other side as she kisses my neck where she licked and sucked.

DJ grins and sucks on my lower lip. His hand moves up just a little on my thigh. He runs his thumb over my jeans but presses against my clit. I jerk into him as my eyes snap open, and I moan into his kiss.

"So, you like that…," he whispers as he cups my pussy and rubs his palm against me. I'm instantly wet for him. He squeezes me as I grip his wrist. He kisses me as Mariah kisses my neck softly. She lets her hand slide down my stomach again.

I inhale sharply when I feel her hand between my thighs. She shifts just slightly and lifts my leg onto hers, spreading me apart a little further. The fabric of my jeans rubbing against my clit with the pressure of DJ's palm makes everything stop. All that I can focus on is DJ's lips on mine. Mariah's on my neck. Her hand moving back up to my tits and pinching my nipples. Their breath on me.

Except it's not my jeans I'm feeling against my clit for long. Seconds after he's started rubbing me, DJ is unbuttoning my jeans and sliding his hands down to my soaked and aching pussy. He groans against my neck as he slides his middle finger into me and rubs my clit with his thumb.

I let my head fall back as my stomach tightens. I moan and arch into both of them as I close my eyes. DJ and Mariah both kiss down my collarbone. Neither of them stop touching me. Rubbing. Pinching.

"Oh… God… Please…" I'm so close to the edge, the peak of my desire, that I don't even care about the people here waiting to celebrate with DJ.

"Please?" DJ rumbles against my neck. I don't know how, but they've both managed to make my body sing for them. I'm trembling. I'm so close to breaking.

"I'm so close," I whimper.

Mariah's hand slides down my stomach to between my thighs. She grips my pussy over my jeans as DJ drives me to madness. Her hand squeezing drives DJ's finger deeper. I buck into them both. Mariah's other hand fists my hair as she kisses me long and deeply.

I grip both of their thighs as I careen closer and closer to the point of no return. My pussy is pulsing erratically. I'm clenching uncontrollably around DJ's finger. Mariah continues squeezing my pussy while DJ expertly thrusts his finger and crooks it against a spot that makes me see stars. He rubs my clit so perfectly with just the right amount of pressure that I can't find my breath.

Mariah pulls slowly away. The heat in her eyes takes my breath away. "You should probably come for us, then," she whispers against my lips.

"Now," DJ rumbles against my neck, sending some kind of sexy vibration through my entire body.

I grip their thighs hard and shatter. "DJ! Mariah! Oh, fuck… Yes!" I close my eyes as DJ and Mariah both help me ride wave after wave of pleasure. I fall backwards, but they both catch me in their waiting arms as I soak my jeans. I feel it on my thighs as I come intensely and harder than I've ever come in my entire life.

When I come down from the high they've brought me to, I'm panting against DJ's shoulder. Both Mariah and DJ are kissing me softly and hugging me tightly. I feel DJ pull his finger out slowly. I whimper at the loss, but my heart stops when he slides his finger into Mariah's waiting mouth. She sucks me off of it as he slowly pulls it out. I watch in complete fascination as he sticks his finger in his mouth and sucks it clean.

My mouth drops slightly as I watch. My stomach clenches tightly again as my pussy pulses erratically. I wouldn't be able to stop the second wave of pleasure when it hits me if I tried to, but when he kisses me and I taste myself on his tongue, I lose all control. I moan as I come a second time. Mariah turns my head to her when DJ pulls away and kisses me just as deeply. I can taste myself on her, too, but it's different. Sweeter.

"Mmm…," I moan as she gently pulls away. I melt into them both when they both wrap their arms around me.

"You know, that second orgasm was sexy as hell. But if you come again without permission, I might have to edge you until you're a writhing mess beneath me." DJ grins teasingly.

Mariah giggles. "It might be kinda fun to see how far we can push you before you lose complete control and scream for us as you beg us to let you come." She kisses my nose."

I giggle and lick my lips with a soft smile. "I might like that," I say quietly.

"We need to stop this before it gets taken to a place you aren't ready for yet, and we miss the entire party downstairs." DJ kisses my cheek as he and Mariah both slowly pull away. DJ leans down and kisses my throat. "Besides. I like you in my clothes and want to see you wearing this shirt a little longer before I rip it off you and let Mariah have her way with you while I watch."

I squeak and blush while moaning slightly. "Fuck me," I whisper with a silent whimper.

"Go change those jeans, though, baby," Mariah says with a pretty blush. "We made you soak them. And while I like the scent of you all sexed up, I have no desire to allow anyone other than us to experience that pretty smell."

I quietly squeak again and blush as I nod. "Yes, ma'am." I quickly grab a different pair of pants and hurry to the bathroom. I change as fast as I can and make my way back to my room.

Mariah and DJ grin a little wickedly as they each take one of my hands and tug me out of my safe place. I tremble a little, but they reassure me by rubbing their thumbs over my hands. They lead me downstairs and to the celebration. Everyone congratulates DJ and Layne. I expect DJ to leave my side to talk to them or something, but he doesn't. Mariah and DJ keep me between them the entire time. When I feel nervous, neither of them push me away when I press myself against them.

As the night goes on, I come to several conclusions, some that I don't know how to interpret. One of them is that ever since the spanking, the demon hasn't uttered a single word. Not even Matt or Luca have been able to do more than muffle her.

Another is that they both made me experience the most intense orgasm I've ever had. I felt so connected to them both. So loved and cherished by them both. No one has ever cared about my feelings or pleasure before.

One of the last things, the biggest one of all, is that I really believe that this could work. No one here seems to think the three of us together is odd. Everyone is treating this like any other relationship. Which makes me believe that, while it's new territory, it can be completely normal.

Everything I've ever wanted.

Somewhere I belong.

Chapter Ten

☆ DJ ☆

(Three Months Later)

I groan sleepily as I blink awake. I look over my shoulder with a yawn and glare at my phone when I see it's vibrating on my nightstand. As carefully as I can, I move my arm out from underneath Mariah's and Lyric's head and smile when they both cuddle closer to each other in their sleep.

I grab my phone and see Matt's number.

Then see the time.

Why the fuck are you calling at four in the damn morning for?

Matt would never do that unless it was something important. Which is why I grab my jeans I draped over the armchair last night and put them on quickly as I'm silently leaving the bedroom. I don't want my girls to wake up unless they need to. Not at this hour.

"What?" I whisper as I answer his third attempt at calling. At least from what I can see. Who knows how many times he called before I woke up.

"Fuck, DJ. I almost started calling Lyric and Mariah," Matt says, breathing a sigh of relief. "Listen, I can't waste time. You have two uniforms on their way to you with an arrest warrant. I don't know how the ever living fuck they got it, but they did. I checked. Someone woke up a judge."

My heart quits pumping. "What?" My head starts spinning. I sit down on a barstool at my kitchen counter. I keep my voice low because Mariah and Lyric aren't the only ones I don't want to wake up. Layne has Beckett over, and I don't want the kids waking up either.

"Yeah. I don't know all the details, man, but I know they're on their way. I just got a call from Emerson. She said the call came out. When she got to the scene, she was told it was under control and to call off. The next thing she knows, a Sergeant is being called."

I shake my head, not following. "She is a Sergeant."

"Yeah. That's what threw her. She called me. She said something wasn't right. The call was to the hospital. The RP?"

My mind can't catch up. "I have no fucking clue."

"Desiree Rens."

I swallow. Hard. I knew he was going to say it. I guess I was just hoping the motherfucker wouldn't. "Christ. What now? And why the fuck is she still going by Rens?"

"Your guess is as good as mine, DJ. I thought she dropped your name."

"She did. I saw the fucking papers. Fuck. I have a copy of them. What's going on Matt? And why the hell does it sound like you're flying at warp speed?"

"Because I am, DJ. Emerson was on the other side of town when I called her back after finding out about the arrest warrant. We're both trying to get to you before they do because something is fucking fishy as hell." He takes a deep breath. "Not only are you like a brother to me, it's also because of Lyric. I know Beckett can take it. I don't want him to see it, but I know he'd jump in and help, just like Layne would. I don't want the kids hurt. Fuck. Mariah would do the same thing. I don't want her hurt either. But my little sister is in that apartment. Violence is a huge trigger for her. The last time a fight broke out near her, she went almost catatonic. It took Luca and I hours to bring her back, and even then she was jumpy for days after. I don't know what these two fucking uniforms are going to do. But

I'm not taking any chances. There's nothing saying they'll follow arrest rules if they're already breaking rules to get the fucking warrant."

I glance down the hallway and swallow again. I can't imagine how any of them would react if they heard a fight going on out here. Which is exactly what I think would happen, whether I cooperate or not. There's no doubt in my mind that Matt is right when he says something about this isn't right. It feels like a huge damn setup, and I'm the one caught in the trap of lies and deceit.

The question is why.

"How close are you?" I ask quietly.

"Close enough. They just called over the radio that they're there. DJ, I'm not kidding. Don't fucking open that door until me and Emerson are on the scene."

I chuckle. "Not a chance in hell. I know I can take them, but I don't want the commotion waking and scaring my family."

"Sit tight. We're pulling in now. I see their squads. Don't see them."

I grumble. "That was fucking fast."

"Probably said they were here after they already got in. I was hoping to head them off. Emerson and I are coming up now."

I hear him pounding up the stairs. I know he's doing it for two reasons. One, cops don't like arriving to calls and taking elevators. We never know what awaits us on the other side of the door. Two, he's hoping those fuckers took the stairs like we would. Good thing Matt is in shape. I live on the top floor. There are four floors in this complex.

Unfortunately, he's not fast enough. I close my eyes and pinch the bridge of my nose. I can hear the uniforms outside my door. I have no doubt in my mind they're gonna bang on it. And as soon as that happens, the kids and my girls are going to wake up.

I do *not* want them to be disturbed by whatever the fuck this newest drama is. I don't want them to be touched by Desiree and her bullshit. Stupid fucking me for thinking we were done with her ass. At least for now. I thought she'd be a good girl and keep her nose clean until after her trial. After that, I expected some bullshit.

I let out a long breath. "They're outside my door," I say quietly, nowhere near loudly enough to alert them I'm even awake or onto them.

"Fourth floor now, DJ. We got your back. Just sit tight." Matt hangs up.

"Thank the fucking devil for Matt Chance," I mumble under my breath. No way God created that asshole. He's too much of a dick.

I chuckle. Truth is, I wouldn't want anyone else on my side. Matt is loyal to a fault when it comes to his family and those close to him. Fuck with any of us, and a wrath worse than that of Satan himself would rain down on their heads. I'm the same. It might be one of the reason's Matt and I have been friends for so fucking long.

I stand when I hear Matt's voice outside my door. He's being pretty quiet, but I can definitely hear the command in his voice; the growl. I grin and lean against the door so I can hear better. I'd open it, but that might be adding fuel to a fire I don't want my family to be a part of.

"I'm your fucking commanding officer," Matt growls. "You're done here."

"Just because he's your fuck buddy or something -" one of the officers says. I bite my lip and grin. That will *not* go over well with Matt.

"Watch… your… fucking… mouth…," Matt says, enunciating each word, effectively cutting the fucker off. "Give me the warrant. You're gone. You both will be in my office at zero-seven-hundred hours. If you are one minute late, you will both face a far worse fate than a fucking suspension. Like termination. I'll make sure of it. Now get the fuck out of here. Now."

There's silence. I smile wider. I know he's watching them sulk to the elevator. He won't make a single move until they're behind the closed doors. He'll glare at them the entire time. I'd almost pay money to see it.

"What the hell is going on, Lieutenant?" Emerson asks Matt quietly.

"Your guess is as good as mine," Matt growls gruffly.

I take the opportunity to open the door. He wouldn't have talked if the uniforms weren't gone. "What's up?" I ask quietly.

"I don't know, man," Matt says as he reads the warrant in his hand. Emerson follows him through the door. Bonnie Emerson has been with GPD nearly as long as I have. She loves her job more than most. It's what makes her such a good cop.

"Just… stay quiet. I don't want anyone woken up," I tell them.

Matt sits down on one of the barstools as he reads. Bonnie follows suit. I grab one and move it to the other side of the counter. I watch them both. Matt sighs and rubs his temples as he reads it. I raise an eyebrow.

He slides the warrant to me. "Desiree is saying that you beat her up. According to that, she has bruising all over her body. It looks like she was tied up. She has been choked. That says there are images taken of her injuries."

I scan the warrant. "How the hell could they prove enough to get a warrant? There's no way they could know it's me based on this bullshit." I toss the warrant on the counter.

"They said they have video," Bonnie says. "The hospital. I guess it shows you dumping her out of a car."

"Well, that's funny. Because I've been here the whole fucking night with my family and my son's boyfriend." I rub my temples. "Whatever they have or whoever they saw isn't me."

"I already sent someone to grab a copy," Matt says. "The Sergeant who responded and the two officers who took the statement have all been called to my office. I'll get to the bottom of it, DJ, but you're going to have to stay far away from this."

"I know the routine." Can't say I fucking like it. "What fucking game is she playing this time?"

"Her trial is on Monday. Or hearing. Whatever the fuck. She's still trying to ruin you. Pretty simple," Matt says.

Bonnie shrugs. "I think she's trying to get a continuance. She knows she's going to jail for what she did. Anything she can do to delay the inevitable and get back at you for being such a horrible husband."

I chuckle at that. Most of the cops I work with know Desiree has been nothing but a pain in my ass for a long time. I've largely left her alone, even though I could have had her charged with filing false police reports years ago.

"Maybe I've been too nice in the not pressing charges thing against her for all of the shit over the years," I say.

"I'd say, Cap. Maybe you really should have been the asshole we all know you as," Bonnie says with a smile.

I grin. "Give her more ammo. Got it." I glance up at the clock. Still very early. I yawn and look back at Matt. "So? What are we doing?"

"You're sitting tight. I have people grabbing the surveillance at the hospital. Unless you have a twin we don't know about, I highly doubt the person who dumped her looks like you. In the meantime, I have them asking her questions. They're on orders from me, so the Sergeant on scene, if he hasn't left yet, has been ranked by me. We'll figure it out."

"Maybe you should go keep those girls warm," Bonnie says with a wink as she stands with Matt.

I give her a tired smile and nod at the arrest warrant. "What about that? Judge's orders."

Matt shrugs and winks. "I'll take care of it. Rescind it. I know some people. Probably more than fucking Sergeant Ricardo."

I raise an eyebrow. "Is that who's on this case?"

"Don't let anyone know I told you that, Cap," Matt says with a grin as he and Bonnie leave.

I stare after them in shock. Sergeant Jose Ricardo is one of the fuckers who were caught banging her. It wasn't on his shift, so he didn't get in near as much trouble as he should have, but I advocated for him to be fired right along with the assholes who were on shift when they showed up at my house and took turns fucking her on my bed.

Now, he's trying to build a fucking case against me?

No. Nope. This isn't happening.

But I know better than to get involved in a case that involves me. Especially when it comes to Desiree.

I sigh and let out a low rumble of a growl as I push my palms against my eyes and rub. "What the fuck is happening?" I ask myself for what I'm sure is the millionth time.

I doubt I'll sleep, but I get up anyway and head back to my bedroom after locking up again. I yawn and contemplate grabbing my gym clothes. Maybe I should head into work early and grab some gym time. We have a nice gym only for officers and staff at the headquarters building. I don't use it often because there's a gym in this building just for residents, but I'm in a vindictive as fuck mood. Walking into HQ without cuffs on my wrists like nothing happened at all and seeing the looks on their faces would be a pretty fucking rewarding way to start my day.

Decision made, I quietly open the door to my bedroom fully intending on leaving my girls a note and grabbing my gym clothes and gear. The plan was to shower at Headquarters, get dressed, then deal with the bullshit day I know is ahead of me.

But as soon as I see what's happening when I slip into the bedroom, all of those plans are quickly tossed into the trash and lit on fire. My mouth drops, and my throat very suddenly feels like I swallowed sand. I completely forget how to breathe, but I thankfully remember to close the door quietly.

And then I watch in complete shock and a little awe.

A lot turned on.

Mariah has a giggling Lyric on her back. Her head is between Lyric's thighs. Her hands are pushing Lyric's legs apart. She's teasing Lyric's pussy with her tongue, making her moan, giggle, and arch.

I palm my instantly hard cock and give myself a couple of squeezes, but it's not enough. I don't want to interrupt what's going on in front of me, but I'm not going to be able to just sit idly by and do nothing. It's far too fucking hot, and I know it's going to make me come.

So, I quietly unbutton my jeans as I watch Mariah become a little more aggressive in her licking. She moans into Lyric's pussy and makes her jerk. I step out of my jeans as I start stroking my dick. I get a little closer but try to stay quiet because I don't want them to stop.

"Oh… Mariah…," Lyric moans as she bucks into Mariah's tongue.

"Mmm…," Mariah moans into Lyric's pussy once more. "Yummy…" Mariah licks faster and starts shaking her head back and forth as her tongue darts in and out of Lyric's pussy.

Unable to stay silent any longer, I groan and make my way to the side of the bed. Still jerking my cock, I reach over and tap Mariah's ass lightly as I watch her vigorously lick and suck on Lyric's soaked pussy. I know exactly how that feels and how she tastes because I've gone down on both of them many times over the past three months. I'll never be able to get my fill of either of them.

They both squeak a little when they see me. I can see Lyric's eyes widen, but Mariah smiles and doesn't stop feeding on Lyric's sweetness. In fact, she becomes relentless. She gets faster. Harder. She licks deeper and swirls her tongue as she shakes her head. Lyric's head falls back, and she moans as she bucks into Mariah's tongue.

"Suck on her clit," I command a little raspily. But I need to see it. I squeeze myself a little harder in anticipation.

"Mmm…," Mariah moans again as she obeys and licks her way to Lyric's clit.

Lyric tangles her fingers in Mariah's hair. "More," she begs. Mariah nips her clit and licks furiously as she moans.

"Give her two fingers," I rumble. My eyes fall to Mariah's hand slowly moving up Lyric's thigh. With no warning, she thrusts two fingers into Lyric's pussy.

Lyric arches and moans, barely holding back a scream. That level of control she portrays at the same time she's losing it, makes me harder. I'm close. I know Lyric is, but I have other plans. I slow my pace on myself as I watch them. Mariah pumps her fingers in and out of Lyric's pussy hard, deep, and fast. I can see her twisting her fingers as she sucks her clit harder and flicks it with her tongue.

"Mariah," Lyric whispers as she bucks underneath her and writhes. "I… please… Mariah, please."

I grin wickedly because something I've learned about both Lyric and Mariah over the past few months is that neither of them can come without the command to do it.

Keeping myself on edge, I lean down. I cup the globe of Mariah's ass. "Tell her to come," I whisper in her ear.

Mariah whimpers and moans at the low dominance of my voice, which was my plan. Her moan vibrates against Lyric's clit, sending her higher. "Come for me, my beautiful angel," she says. There's a hint of dominance there, but not nearly as much as me.

It's enough to make Lyric slap one hand over her mouth and tug Mariah close to her pussy, though. "Ah! Mariah!" Lyric screams into her hand. Her hips jerk as she comes and rides her high. Mariah doesn't stop until Lyric has collapsed in pleasure underneath her and stopped spasming.

"Fuck," I whisper as I watch. I squeeze my dick harder when my own release gets dangerously close. "Come here." I take a couple of steps back. "Kneel." That raspiness is back. Fuck, these two are beautiful.

Both of them scurry to the end of the bed with their eyes hungrily on my cock. They kneel in front of me with their legs slightly spread and their palms resting on their thighs. I don't know when the hell they started doing that, but I didn't realize that I needed it. It appeals to the true dominant in me I'm not totally sure I knew existed. I've always known I was an Alpha male. But fuck. Nothing like what they turn me into.

They both tilt their heads back and stick out their tongues. And that right there is all it takes. I can't hold back anymore. I stroke myself faster until I'm just about to come, then I feed my cock to Lyric. Her warm mouth closes over it, and the wetness of her tongue darting over my tip sends me over the edge. I tangle my fingers in her hair and slide deeper, until I'm touching the back of her throat, and come. Hard.

"Holy fuck, baby," I groan as she swallows around me and drinks my come like water. I'd never allow myself to leave my other girl out, so I slowly pull my dick out of Lyric's mouth and hold myself back from finishing only long enough for Mariah to take me in her mouth. When she closes her lips around me, she instantly starts sucking. "Oh fuck, Rih."

I almost lose my balance and tumble into her when she starts swallowing my come just as greedily as Lyric had been seconds before. Instead, I tangle my fingers in her hair and let my head fall back.

When I finish and start gently pulling out, Lyric and Mariah both start licking me clean. I look down at them. Neither of them know how sexy it is to watch them both licking my cock. I almost come again, but reality sets in when my alarm to wake up goes off. I reach over to the night stand and shut it off as they finish lavishing my cock.

I help them both up. Their huge smiles could light the room even more than the sun would if I had the shades open. I really hate that I'm about to be the motherfucker that wipes those beautiful looks from their faces.

I sit down with a sigh and pull them both down so they're sitting in my lap, one on each thigh. I keep an arm tightly around each of them. "We need to talk…," I begin.

And just like I knew it would, the serious tone of my voice wipes that brightness off their lips. I've cursed Desiree a lot over the past few years, the last year especially.

But this.

This is so far beyond the laws of sanity. I don't know her game. I don't know why the fuck she'd ever think to do this.

All I know is my girls need to know what's happening…

… and I hate every single fucking second of it…

Chapter Eleven

☆ Mariah ☆

The dreaded words.

We need to talk.

And they just came out of my boyfriend's mouth.

I look at Lyric when I hear a sharp intake of breath. Her eyes immediately fall to her hands, which are fisted into each other as she wrings them. She sucks her lip into her mouth, and her shoulders slump. I know without her saying anything that she's thinking exactly what I am. That her demon is saying exactly what mine is.

Told you. Stupid fool. Told you this wouldn't last. He just wanted sex. He doesn't need you to get that. He can find someone so much prettier than you.

I close my eyes and fight against him as hard as I can. I try to shove him away. DJ would never do that. He thinks I'm beautiful. That we both are. He tells us all the time. I hold my breath and tell my demon just that.

But he doesn't listen. He laughs. Like my pain is hysterical. And it is to him. He feeds off it. *Stupid girl. Look at you compared to her. Lyric's everything you aren't. Of course he'd pick her over you.*

"You're breaking up with me," Lyric whispers so quietly that I'm not sure the words even actually left her mouth or if I imagined them. She slowly gets up. "I'll leave," she says just as quietly.

My heart starts pounding out of my chest. I look between her and DJ frantically, but my breathing is trying to compensate for the sudden uptick in my blood pressure. Instead, I hug myself and tremble. Tears sting my eyes.

"What?" DJ asks in shock. He's not quick enough to catch her, though. She flees to the other side of the room where she neatly folded her jeans and starts putting them on.

"I'm sorry. I m-must have d-done so-something." She swallows hard as she sniffles.

"DJ?" I'm finally able to whisper.

He glances at me and shakes his head, bewildered. "Lyric, stop, honey. That's not -"

"It was too good t-to be tr-true," she sobs as she shakes her head and buttons her jeans. "I sh-should've kn-known. I'm s-sorry. I didn't m-mean to ruin an-anything for you."

"DJ?" I squeak a little louder. I dig my nails into my sides.

"Baby, what are you talking about? Ruin -"

"I sh-should've known." She sobs harder as she fumbles with her shirt. "I-I'm not g-good enough. A-Always the f-fuck u-up... I-I'm n-never good e-enough..."

DJ nudges me up and sets me on the bed as I watch everything unfolding in both shock and horror. I don't know what's happening. I can't comprehend it.

See? Idiot. Told you he'd choose her. Look at her. She's everything he wants. So much more submissive than you. She knows how to please him. She knows what a man like that wants.

I cover my ears and close my eyes. "No," I whisper sob to myself as I shake my head.

I slide down to the floor. Through my tears, I can see DJ holding Lyric tightly and swaying with her. He's whispering to her as she clings to him. I curl into myself, keeping my hands over my ears. I know what he's doing. I heard her words. I know he's reassuring her. I know that. But I can't stop it. I can't shut the demon up.

You're the one who isn't good enough. Never have been.

"I am," I whisper.

He doesn't need you. He has her.

"No…" I shake my head and tremble. I know he wants us both. We've been planning our future together. With all of us. He tells us all the time how happy he is. We all tell each other how perfect this is.

So stupid for believing he'd want you both. How complicated is that? And you think she'd want you? When she has him? I can physically feel him rolling his fictional eyes.

"No…," I whisper again. *I won't let you take control,* I tell him. I try harder to push him away, but it's like I'm pushing against an invisible but impenetrable wall. *I won't let you beat me!*

I've worked too hard to let him do this to me again. To let him send me to the hospital again. To give me such a bad panic attack that I need to be admitted again. I won't let him do that to me. Not this time. I squeeze my eyes tighter and make myself breathe. My chest feels like it's being squeezed with a clamp. Like my chest is going to collapse at any second. Like my lungs have been punctured.

But I won't let him beat me.

Not again.

"No…," I whisper.

He laughs. I can hear him. *Stupid girl. You're losing everything.*

"No!" I scream.

"Mariah? Look at us, baby," I hear DJ say. His voice cuts through the darkness I'm fighting my way out of. He and Lyric both drop in front of me as my eyes fly open.

"Mariah?" Lyric touches my knee lightly. Shakily. But her touch and sweetness and DJ's soothing scent and voice envelops me. It's like that invisible wall has shattered into a million tiny shards that are raining down on me as I reach the light I was grasping for.

Them.

My light.

I watch them both, unsure.

DJ reaches up and wipes my tears, then kisses me softly. "I don't know what that fucking demon said to you just now, but he's wrong, baby," DJ whispers against my lips. "I'm not leaving you. We're not breaking up. The three of us are in this forever. We already decided that. None of us have ever had a connection with anyone else like we do with each other. We're not fucking losing that." He kisses me again. "So, the demon can take a leap into shark infested waters, sweet girl. Because I'm not going anywhere."

"Me either," Lyric whispers, shakily. "There's nowhere I would rather be…," she whispers with a sniffle. She glances at DJ before looking down at her hands. "I t-thought y-you were b-breaking up w-with m-me…," she cuts off on a sob and bites her lip.

DJ wraps his arms around us both. "No one is breaking up with anyone. I know where you both got that. I shouldn't have started out with the dreaded 'we need to talk' phrase. I know better than that." He pulls away slowly and kisses us both, but keeps his arms around us as we all hug each other on the floor.

After a few moments, though, DJ stands and guides us both to the bed. He glances at the clock and sighs, then ushers us both into bed. He crawls between us and pulls the blanket up as he leans against the headboard.

"I don't have a lot of time. I need to leave for work soon, but a little while ago, Matt called," DJ begins. Lyric and I both cuddle closer and lay our head on his chest. We link pinkies over his washboard abs.

"What happened?" I ask quietly.

DJ's arms tighten around us both. His muscles flex with tension. "Desiree. She ended up in the hospital last night."

"Oh no," Lyric whispers. We both look up at him.

DJ closes his eyes and rubs his hands up and down our arms slowly. "She was beat up. I know nothing more than that right now, but she accused me of doing it." His voice is low and growly as he slowly opens his eyes. There isn't a ton of light in here, but it's obvious his have darkened. He's pissed.

"Wait, what?" Lyric furrows her brows. "How? You weren't with her."

DJ nods. "Exactly. I have an alibi. But some shit went down and a couple of officers were sent to arrest me this morning. Another Sergeant smelled something was off and contacted Matt. He interceded and stopped it all from happening, but that doesn't really solve the problem we have going on here."

I sigh and slump against him when I realize what's happening. "Someone on the force set you up."

"Not just someone. We have a Sergeant for sure. Probably two uniforms."

"Uniforms…?" Lyric asks hesitantly.

"Patrol officers, beautiful girl," DJ explains. "The ones who respond to calls for service. We call them uniforms or patrol." He kisses the top of their head. "Matt has a meeting with them, but he's gathering as much information as he can first. I know in the arrest warrant they said they have video of me pushing her out of my vehicle and speeding away. They have her statement of what happened. I didn't see much more than that, so I don't know what time this all happened." DJ glances at his phone on the nightstand, then reaches for it. "It's Matt." He puts it on speaker. "Matt. You're on speaker. What'd you find out?"

"First of all," Matt begins. DJ shifts a little so he can still hug us and hold the phone. "The girls and kids. They okay?"

"Boys are sleeping. The girls are okay. Little bit of a scare, but we worked through it. I said we needed to talk. They both thought we were breaking up."

Matt chuckles. "No way that's happening. Y'all are way too much in love. Anyway, listen. I don't have much time. I'm leaving the hospital. On my way to HQ. That video. It's not you at all. I'm positive they intended to cover it somehow, but it was the two uniforms that were serving your arrest warrant. The hospital gave them a copy. They still had the original footage. They ran me a copy and themselves, just in case those assholes get their copy to a specialist or something and have some voodoo tech shit happen and superimpose your face or some crap on it. The car isn't yours. It's a white Grand Prix. The plate comes back to Keith Morgan."

DJ furrows his brows. "Officer Keith Morgan?"

"Yep. He was driving. Mitchell Jones was the one in the passenger seat. He's the one who shoved her out. You can see them speed away. There's no audio, but I think they blared the horn because as soon as a nurse started running out, they took off. Desiree looked like she was pretty beat up. I did talk to her…" He trails off.

I look at the phone then at DJ and Lyric. It's Lyric who takes a deep breath and finally speaks. "What did she say?" she asks.

Matt lets out a breath. "At first, she stuck to her story. Then she told me that Ricardo threatened her. He told her that it was her fault she was in the hospital, but she's not going to point her, and I quote, slutty fingers at him or any of his buddies." Matt sighs. "I have to get the full story. I'm pulling in that fucker Ricardo and his two buddies. I'm not confident they'll show up, though, so I have some guys waiting for them to haul them in as soon as they show up at the garage with their squads. I do think they'll be cocky enough to at least do that. Their vehicles are parked in the police garage. If not, well, I have enough for an arrest warrant myself. I'll get it and go hunting."

"Maybe you shouldn't go in today," I say quietly.

"No, Rih. DJ needs to come in. He needs to be business as usual," Matt says. "He can't touch this case, but he needs to come in and show everyone that he's not the fucked up one."

"I don't want you to go," Lyric whispers.

"I know, baby," DJ says quietly. "But Matt's right. I need to go about this like any other day and let him do what he needs to do. I still don't know what her plan was in this. Or theirs, if what she's saying is true."

"I have to be honest, Cap," Matt says before I can open my mouth. "You won't hear me say this ever again, but I believe her on this one. I think she was threatened. She said she had a few people over. Things got hot and heavy. And then it wasn't hot anymore. I don't want to say too much with the girls there, but I don't think she'd lie about this. I think they were covering their asses when things got out of hand."

I can feel Lyric trembling. We've all been adjusting to our new relationship, and I know she trusts that DJ would never do something like this, but she was beat up by one of her exes. I know just hearing what DJ is being accused of has shaken her to her core. I have no doubt that she wants to run.

DJ, thankfully, feels it, too. "Matt, cover for me. I know what I should do, but Lyric is struggling. So is Rih. I can't leave them like this. Maybe I'll be in later. I don't know. Just keep me updated. Tell me what you need."

Matt chuckles. "Lily. Are you listening to me?"

"Yes, sir," Lyric whispers.

"What happened to you in no way shape or form dictates your future. You know that, honey. DJ is a good guy. He's not like your ex. You need to fight that doubt and fear off and trust him. You know he didn't do this. And you know he wouldn't. Okay?"

"Okay," she whispers to him.

"We're all in for a long day, Cap. Take care of my sisters. I'm fine with Beckett staying home today." Matt pauses. "I gotta go. I'll call you later. I'll cover for you."

"Thanks, Matt." DJ hangs up and snuggles us closer.

"I don't want to say this, but you have to show your face at some point today…," Lyric says after several moments of silence and soaking up DJ's strength and love. "Or you'll look guilty. I don't want you to go in, but… you have to…"

"Baby, I'm not leaving either of you in this state," DJ says protectively and dominantly. "Mariah may seem okay, but she's still shaken. And I know damn well you are. I can feel it. You're trembling. You're scared. You want to flee because of what happened to you. You feel like you're a burden on me by staying here because I need to be concentrating on getting myself out of this, but you're very, very wrong, beautiful girl. Matt will do what needs to be done. No one is going to be upset with me for not showing up today. Will they think I'm guilty? Maybe, but very doubtful. Especially when Matt is finished with those assholes."

I take a breath and close my eyes as I shift and sit up with my back against the headboard next to DJ. I play with the edge of the blanket. "I think she's right, DJ," I say carefully. "They could do a lot of damage if you don't go in. And… maybe Lyric needs to go home. Not because I want her to. I don't. But her sanctuary is her room in Matt's house. Just like mine is the chair by my window. Maybe we just… need to be in our safe places."

DJ sighs and shifts so he's sitting up more. He helps Lyric so she's sitting up but is curled into his side with her legs thrown over his. I grip her ankle, rubbing my thumb soothingly across it as he rubs her leg soothingly.

"Listen. Both of you," DJ begins. "I understand that for years you've both had your own corners of the world to retreat to. And I know that's where you both want to go right now. But I have four problems with that. The first is that I know you both better than that. I'll take Lyric home after getting you settled in your apartment. The boys will stay here and take a day to come down after I tell them what happened."

"DJ -" I begin softly.

"No, let me finish. You both will retreat to those safe places and fight all day long with your demon. By the time the day is over, I'll have lost so much footing and improvement we've worked towards with both of your anxiety that we'll have to start completely over from the bottom. I am *not* willing to allow either of you to sink into that dark place and allow the demon in your mind to get the better of you. It's not going to happen. And the second is that the entire time I'm gone, I'll be obsessing over both of you and wondering how you're doing. Nothing will get done. The better option for all of us is to stay here, as a family, which is what we are. Allow Matt to do his job without me getting in his way, which I would do. Third, you both are very action-oriented. You need me to prove through my actions that everything is going to be okay. But mostly, that we are going to be okay. And last is that I want your safe place, your sanctuary, to be with me. In my apartment. I want you both to consider my place yours. I don't want either of you running off to somewhere else when you need to decompress. I want you to feel safe here."

"Then, a compromise?" Lyric says timidly.

"I'm up for negotiation. How's that?" DJ says with a smile as he kisses her forehead. I reach for her hand. He might say he's up for a negotiation, but it will always be DJ's way.

"You go in for half the day. Because you have to, DJ," she says as she squeezes my hand. "Mariah and I will stay here. We'll... work or something. We'll stay occupied. The boys will be here. That will help."

"No deal. Because I'll still be worried as hell about you both and wondering if I'm going to come back to an empty apartment and the loves of my life in a state of panic that is bound to scare me."

I have to chuckle at her squeak at his declaration. I don't need to look at her to know she's flushed a pretty pink. Just as pink as I'm sure my cheeks are.

"Then, you'll check in every hour on the hour," Lyric says, and I'm impressed by her skills. I've never been able to get DJ to budge on anything when he's made a decision, and I've always considered myself a pretty good negotiator.

After a few moments, DJ sighs, and I feel him relent. "Fine. A half day. That's all you're getting out of me. And if you don't answer when I call, that's it. I'm coming home."

My mouth drops. "Well, damn. How did you do that? I've never been able to do that."

"I must be getting soft in my old age," DJ teases. "Okay. Fine. Let me take a shower. You both go get the boys up."

"I think Mariah should do that…," Lyric says softly. "They have a habit of ignoring me when I do. Last time, Beckett screamed at me to get out and leave him the fuck alone to sleep. Ended up with a huge punishment from Matt, but it stuck with me." She sits up slowly. "I'll make us all breakfast and pack something for you to take in with you."

"Lyric, it wasn't a suggestion. It was an order. If they give you shit, it will be dealt with. You're just as much an authority figure as me and Mariah are. Now go. Both of you. Get dressed. Get the boys up. Then you both can make breakfast, but neither of you are to be alone. And that…" He kisses us both in turn. Deeply. "Is non-negotiable."

Lyric and I both watch him as he climbs out of bed. Neither of us say anything as he struts to the bathroom. He turns on the light and doesn't bother to close the door. Moments later, we hear the shower running and both burst into giggles.

"He's paying for that order," Lyric mutters between giggles as she crawls out of bed. "I'm wearing his sweats and a hoodie… with no panties."

My eyes widen. "You little devil." I follow her out of bed. "But it's a really good idea, and I'm totally copying you. Not even a little bit ashamed."

"And maybe I'll soak them with my come for good measure." She giggles and slips on the sweats after stripping off her jeans. "The punishment would be worth it."

I laugh as we both get dressed. Truthfully, the laughing feels amazing after what just happened. I hate that we both gave into the darkness we suffer from and automatically thought the worst when DJ said we needed to talk, but I'm really happy thinking about how we all got through it.

Together.

Just as it should always be.

Just as it will always be.

Chapter Twelve

☆ Lyric ☆

(Three Days Later)

"DJ?" a soft and very hesitant voice whispers.

I look up and see Desiree standing several feet away. She looks a lot worse for the wear than she did when I first saw her in the courtroom a few months ago. Her blond hair is down. It's not nearly as done up as it was before. Her makeup is light, barely noticeable. Which is ironic since it was so perfect last time. My how the mighty have fallen.

I haven't seen her at all since that day, and that's been completely intentional on my part. If I'm at Matt's and Luca's, I take my walk still, but I don't walk the same path I used to. Not to say I'm there often. Most of my time since the three of us got together has been spent with Mariah and DJ.

"What, Desiree?" DJ asks tiredly. It's more than obvious he's exhausted. Through with all of her shenanigans. Pissed from everything we found out this weekend. Just… worn out.

"Can we… t-talk?" She swallows. Hard. So do I, but mine is the bile rising from my stomach at the thought of this woman being anywhere near the people I love.

DJ makes a hand gesture in the air. "So, talk."

"I… meant alone…," she whispers.

"Des, I have nothing to say to you. At all. The only reason I'm here is because I have to be. Layne, Mariah, and Lyric have to be. So, whatever you need to say, say it."

Desiree watches us all. I glance up at her but don't raise my head. The sadness and regret I see in her eyes, though, surprises me. It's not something I thought I'd see from the woman who has caused both DJ and Layne so much strife. And as much as I want to, I'm not sure I believe it.

She closes her eyes a moment and lets out a breath as she nods, then opens them again. "I just wanted to let you and Layne know that I'm changing my plea," she says softly as she looks down. "To guilty."

"Good. You damn well should," DJ says, his voice devoid of emotion.

Desiree wraps her arms around herself as she smiles softly, but sadly, and looks at Layne. My heart beats a little faster. I don't want her looking at Layne. I don't want her near him. I don't want her to talk to him. None of us do.

"I want you to know that I am sorry," she tells him as she clears her throat. "What I did was wrong. I know that now. I know I can't take it back, though I wish I could. And I know that an apology isn't enough. I hope that one day you might be able to forgive me, but I understand if you don't. And I promise you that I won't be upset about it."

Layne keeps his head down and says nothing. Beckett continues to rub Layne's back as he hugs him. Matt and Luca stand off to the side of us all. They were talking, but as soon as they heard Desiree, they moved closer to us. DJ hasn't moved from my side. He's still holding my hand and soothingly rubbing his thumb in circles on the top of my hand. Mariah, though she's on the other side of me, feels like she's miles away.

I hear Layne sniffle and watch with wide eyes as he angrily stands and swipes a hand across his eyes. DJ abruptly stands as well, letting go of my hand for the first time since we got out of his car, and grabs Layne's arm with a look of warning. Desiree takes a few steps back.

Layne turns to him and puts a hand on his chest. "Dad. I'm fine. It's fine."

DJ slowly lets go of Layne's arm, but he stays rooted to the spot he stands. "Just -"

Layne gives him a small smile. "I'm fine." I watch him turn to a slightly terrified Desiree.

I suppose I can see why she'd be fearful. Layne is tall for a fourteen year old. And he's fairly muscular as well. It's from his love of playing basketball and swimming in his spare time. But the biggest reason she's freaked out is a reason I understand all too well. The bruises give her away.

We found out over the weekend that Desiree had invited three of her previous flings over to her house for a night of what she considered fun and games. Games that included snorting some type of drug and having sex on every surface of her house. And since she has a fondness for recording it all, she had evidence of the entire encounter.

When it went downhill and got a lot more violent than she wanted it to, she tried to put a stop to it. But the three guys had lost control by that time. They were high on drugs and drunk from the sex and alcohol. Not to mention the lust they all felt for the woman allowing them all to fuck her.

I shiver at the images. I didn't see the recording, but Matt told us about them and everything that happened on them, trying to be mindful of me the entire time, when he came over for dinner Saturday night. There was so much stuff that happened, I'm still trying to wrap my head around it.

I let out a breath when Mariah wraps her arms around me and lays her head on my shoulder. I lean my head on hers, and we both melt into each other. For a few moments at least, everything that happened over the weekend takes a backseat to the present moment.

"Desiree," Layne begins as he stops in front of her. I can tell DJ is coiled and ready to intervene if something happens. So is Matt and Luca. It gives me the confidence I need that everything is going to be okay. That Layne is.

"Layne," Desiree whispers as she looks up at him. She's obviously hurt that he called her by her first name, but I can't help the little twinge of pride I feel at it. "I'm really sorry."

"I know. And I do forgive you. Not for you. For me. But I'll never forget what happened. Not just the hit. Or the scratch. I won't forget the drugs. I won't forget the alcohol. I won't forget the times you screamed at dad and went after him. Violently. I won't forget how he stood there and took it all. How he'd wrap his arms around you when you cried and screamed at him. I won't forget the pain on his face or in my heart every time he sat there on the floor with you while you went into a manic, alcohol and drug induced fit of rage. How he tried to help you. Protect you. I won't forget the cops coming to the house and questioning him when it was you who started it all. When he did nothing but try to save you from yourself."

"Layne, I -"

Layne shakes his head and cuts her off. "I won't forget the heartbreak I felt knowing that not only did I have a broken home, but that the woman I once loved more than anything hated me simply because I existed." Layne's words get a little more vicious. Mariah and I hug each other tighter. Not out of fear though. Out of pride for him. Our boy. "I'll never forget every shot you took at me. How you always told me that I ruined your life. That you'd be so much happier with dad if I never came into the world. How you should have aborted me. I'll never forget the day he left. How I begged and pleaded with him to take me with him. I'll never forget the lies you told to get the right to some kind of custody of me during the divorce and custody hearing. A child you yourself stated so many times that you hated. I'll never forget every time you had people over at the house while I was there. How I had to sneak out and go to Beckett's because of it. And you didn't give a crap whether I was there or not. How it was always all about money and what you felt entitled to."

Desiree sniffles and wipes her eyes. "I deserve that. All of it. But - "

"No. No buts," Layne continues. "I'll never forget any of it. But I will forgive it and move on with my life. Why? Because *I deserve it*. I *deserve* the happiness. I *deserve* a fulfilling life." He turns slightly and meets mine and Mariah's eyes. My heart fills with instant love. He gives us both a soft smile before turning back to Desiree. "I *deserve* the love of a mother. A real one. Lucky for me, dad found two amazing women who not only love him in a way he *deserves* to be, a way you *never* did, but they love me in a way that every mother should love her child. So, I *forgive* you, Desiree. But I will never *forget* it. Any of it. I don't want to see you. I don't want to hear from you. I want absolutely nothing to do with you. I hope you get help. You need it. And I hope you find love. True love. Everyone deserves it. I hope you find fulfillment in your life. And I wish all things good for you. Because it's what we all *deserve*. I'm sorry for what happened to you. I hate seeing you standing here bruised and broken. But I'm *done* with you."

Layne turns away from her and ambles back to us with his hands in his pockets. We move apart as he sits between us with his head down and jaw ticking. We both hug him close and tight because that's what he needs.

"I understand, Layne," Desiree says softly. He doesn't look up at her, but Mariah does. Like DJ, she levels her with a vicious glare. I don't need to look up to see it. I can feel it. I keep my focus on Layne, trusting DJ and Mariah to deal with her. She takes a deep breath. "I hope one day you'll change your mind, but if you don't, just know that I am sorry." She turns her focus to DJ. "And thank you. For all you did over the weekend. I knew if I pointed a finger at you, you'd fix everything. You always fixed everything," she whispers.

DJ shakes his head. "You almost got me arrested!" he hisses. He's not yelling, but the venom in his voice causes her to jump a little. Good. "All you had to do was call me, Desiree. You could have told me what was happening."

"They threatened me!" she whisper yells so her voice doesn't echo off the walls. "They told me if I said anything to anyone, they would kill me, then go after you and Layne!"

"And all you had to do was call me up and tell me! You know I would have helped you! All the fucking shit you put me and Layne through aside, I wouldn't have let you suffer like that!" DJ whisper yells right back.

Desiree flinches. "I know. I'm sorry, DJ. Okay? I should have… I should have thought clearer. I was fucked up."

"Like Layne said, Des. I hope you get the help you need. And I'm glad you're owning up to your fucking actions and not putting anyone I love through a needless trial. I hope that this is the turning point for you, and that you can live your life to the full potential I know you have in you. I hope you can lean on your parents to get you through this. Maybe check into a rehab facility. Then start your life over. But we won't be in it."

"State versus Desiree Camden," a bailiff says as he comes out.

DJ chuckles and shakes his head. "So you really did give a false name on the police report. I bet that was all intentional. Something more to get a judge to look at it and see your name was the same as mine and think we're still married. The spousal abuse charge in that arrest warrant makes sense now. Fuck, Desiree." DJ turns away from her. I look up when he stops in front of us and holds out both hands. "We don't need to go in there if you don't want to."

"We want to," Layne answers for us all as Mariah and I take DJ's hands. "We want the closure and conclusion to a very messed up saga. At least I do."

DJ pulls both me and Mariah to our feet. Layne stands and makes his way to Beckett. Matt and Luca follow them into the courtroom. DJ keeps us both back for a few moments as he takes a deep breath. Mariah and I look up at him.

"How are you both holding up?" he asks. His thumb strokes the back of our hands.

"Proud," Mariah whispers. "Relieved. I'm not totally sure I'm okay, but I'm getting there. I just want this chapter in our lives put behind us."

"I'm proud, too," I say softly. I look up at DJ. "But I also don't believe she'll change. No matter what she says, I don't trust it." I take a deep breath knowing they probably won't agree with me. I'm kind of cynical that way. "I know fear, DJ. I know pain. I know desperation. I know how it feels to be on that ledge and teetering… about to fall." I shake my head, glancing at Layne apologetically when he stops before going into the courtroom. He gives us both a look of confusion when he sees we aren't behind them. I look back to DJ. "I saw none of that in her eyes. She may be sorry. But she's more sorry she got caught." I hug myself with one arm since he's still holding my hand. "The other thing I saw? Triumph. Because even if she is going to spend some time in jail, she got what she wanted. She's safe from the men who hurt her. And when she gets out in a couple months? She gets to do that with a clean slate. Do I think she could change? I'm not sure. I hope for everyone's sake she does. I just don't want her to hurt you anymore."

Mariah smiles softly and lets go of DJ's hand. "I'll see you both in there," she says quietly.

I watch her as she slips quietly into the courtroom in front of Layne. "Did I upset her?" I immediately feel bad. I start twisting my fingers. Maybe I shouldn't have said anything. It's not really my place to have an opinion. I don't know anything other than what I've heard recently. Maybe Mariah disagrees with me completely. She knows her a lot more than I do.

"No, baby. Mariah has her own demons. Demons she hasn't even completely opened up to me about." He looks after her, something like sadness crossing over his eyes, then looks back at me with a soft smile. "I agree with you." He leans down and kisses me softly. "I can't really believe that she's going to change. I think she might be sorry. Probably sorry her game is over, too. But I also can't be sure that she's truly just going to turn over a new leaf." He glances back over his shoulder. "We should get in there. Layne will need us."

I nod and follow submissively behind him, holding tightly to his hand. He sits between me and Mariah and pulls us both close. Layne sits with Beckett stoically in the pew in front of us, and I look questioningly at DJ.

"Should we not be with him?" I ask, confused.

"He wanted to sit with Beckett by himself," Mariah says quietly with a soft smile. "He wants to show her that he's able to face her on his own."

I nod again and smile softly. I'm even more proud of Layne, who is becoming such a good young man. My young man. Ours. I feel overflowing joy at getting to call him my own, but even more so at his declaration in the corridor.

His acceptance.

✫✫✫

DJ continues to watch me skeptically as he drives. "You're seriously not going to tell me what's going on?"

I giggle. "Nope! I've been planning this for days."

DJ laughs as he glances in the rearview mirror. The smile falls from his face, and I look back at Mariah. I bite my lip and look out the window. I know she's struggling, but DJ and I can't get her to open up. I just wish we knew what's happening. It makes me wonder... does she regret us...? I close my eyes, shaking my head, and take a deep breath.

"Rih? Did she spill the beans to you?" DJ asks Mariah. Mariah says nothing. It's almost like she doesn't even hear him. I glance back at her worriedly. He reaches behind him and squeezes her knee. "Baby?"

"Hmm...?" She blinks a few times.

"What's going on in that pretty head of yours, beautiful?"

She shakes her head. "Nothing," she says tiredly as she rubs her eyes. "I just haven't slept well. It's messing with me."

"I know the feeling." I turn and give her a bright smile. I shove away all the dark thoughts trying to push through. Not now. I can deal with it later. "But... I have just the thing to make it all better. I packed your favorite bikini. I guilted Matt into making your favorite food on the grill tonight, even though he planned steak."

"Ah ha!" DJ exclaims teasingly. "We're going to Matt's. I knew it!"

I just pout. "Not fair. You weren't meant to be paying attention. You were just meant to be following my directions."

He laughs as he squeezes Mariah's knee again before letting her go. "Is that why you took us in a big loop instead of the straight shot way to his house?"

I stick out my tongue. "Ruin my fun. I had this all mapped out. You still had three turns to get through."

He laughs again as I turn around in the seat. DJ makes a left I hadn't planned and drives to Matt's and Luca's. Mariah falls silent once more, but at least there's a soft smile on her pretty lips.

When DJ pulls in Matt's driveway, my smile grows a little brighter. I open the door and jump out, stumbling a little but catching myself. I open the back door of DJ's car for Mariah. She steps out slowly, then grabs my hand and DJ's. She looks up at us with so much sadness and fear in her eyes that it startles me. I gasp.

"Please... don't hate me... but I can't have kids," she whispers. "I shouldn't have kept it from you for so long." The words coming out of her mouth are like word vomit. Like she can't stop now that she's started. All DJ and I can do is stare at her in shock. "But when I was molested, he left a lot of damage. Scar tissue. I did actually get pregnant once, but I miscarried. I was relieved because I didn't want kids. I felt like an awful person for feeling that way. Who feels relief at a miscarriage? But I did. Then I found out afterwards from my doctor that the pregnancy, if I carried to full term, would have been high-risk. It's unlikely I would have ever been able to carry to term, but if I had, there was little chance that both me and the baby would have survived the birth." She shutters. "I'm sorry I never told you." She looks up at DJ with tears in her eyes before they fall on me. I'm so startled by the admission, I can't even speak.

DJ pulls her into us both. "Rih, first and foremost, I've known for a long time you didn't want kids. So has Lyric. You've always been upfront about that. We didn't know about the other shit, but it changes nothing at all. If that's what this entire thing has been about and why you've been so worried and quiet today, you can put it aside." He nods towards the house. "We already have a pretty amazing kid. You know I had a vasectomy. And you know Lyric refuses to even consider having a child. You know it's because she miscarried as well and can't go through that pain again because it almost killed her." He hugs us both tighter.

"Mariah," I whisper into her hair. I take a shaky breath and bury my face in her neck as I hug her tighter. "That was the silliest thing to be upset about in the entire history of silly things. I hate that you went through all you did, but if you're afraid that we're going to be upset because you can't have kids, then don't be. It doesn't make us love you less." I take another deep breath. I know what her demon is saying to her. I've had the same fight with my own. "And it doesn't make you any less of a woman. You're still beautiful. You're still loved. And you're still ours."

She sniffles and slowly stops shaking. She lifts her head slowly as she nods. She kisses DJ deeply as he hugs her. I smile as I watch them. I can see how whatever the demon was telling her about this is being circumvented by me and DJ. It makes my heart lift with happiness.

My eyes widen when she slowly pushes me against DJ's car and crashes her lips against mine in a kiss that's fiery, all-consuming, deep, and passionate. My toes curl. I'm so wrapped up in her, I don't even realize that my hands have found their way to her hips, or that my eyes have closed. I pull her against me as she grinds her leg between my thighs. I gasp when she hits all the right spots.

"As much as I'd love to watch you fuck our girl right here in this driveway," DJ rumbles low enough for only us to hear. My eyes flutter open as Mariah continues her sudden attack on my pussy. "We should probably head inside and see what Lyric has done to surpr-"

"Dad! Mom! Come look! It's awesome!" Layne comes running up to us and grabs DJ and Mariah's hands in his. He starts tugging them along behind him. I follow them with a secretive smile as they both glance back at me. "You have to see this! It's so cool!" Layne says excitedly. "There's water and foam and bubbles. It's huge!"

He pulls them through the house to the backdoor that leads into Matt's and Luca's huge backyard. I lean against the counter of the kitchen and smile softly as I watch them. Layne keeps tugging DJ and Mariah until they're just a few steps from the surprise I organized. They can't see it yet because of the shades being closed on the sliding glass door.

"What's going on, buddy?" DJ asks.

"This. This is going on." He drops both of their hands and opens the shades with a huge flourish. "Tahdah!" He turns back with wide eyes.

"Holy shit," Mariah says in awe as she looks back at me. "What did you do? How? It's incredible."

I giggle. "I've been saving up all of the money I've been making on covers and designing. I wanted to do something special. So, this is what I did. I couldn't think of anything better than giving those I love a day of fun after so much stress."

Layne rushes to me and hugs me hard, making me squeak as I hug him back. "Thank you! Thank you! Thank you! Mom, you're the best!"

I blush and hide in his shoulder. He's only fourteen and already towers over me. "You're welcome," I say softly.

"Hurry! Get changed! Everyone is already having a ball!" Layne runs out of the house and towards where Beckett is calling for him. I laugh when I see Beckett doing a victory dance. Going by Matt's expression, he just lost some kind of challenge against his son. He's not living that down.

"Shoot. I forgot the bag in the car with our swim stuff." I turn and dart for the door, but DJ catches me.

"How about you let Mariah finish you off? I'll grab the clothes." He spins me and taps my ass as he heads for the door.

I moan softly at Mariah's hungry look. She bites her lip and eyes me. Before I have a second to react, she's taking my hand and tugging me upstairs to my bedroom. The bedroom I'm slowly starting to understand isn't my sanctuary anymore.

My safe place is with Mariah and DJ.
They're my home.

Chapter Thirteen

☆ DJ ☆

I prop my feet up on the table in front of me and sip my coffee. CNN plays quietly in the background as I read the paper. This is one of the few times in my day that I have all to myself. Even my gym time is spent with others most of the time.

It didn't used to be like that. I had a very nice home gym that I spent a lot of time making just right. It was where I went when Desiree pissed me off. Layne liked it, too. It was quiet. I can't even count how many times I'd found him down there when he was supposed to be in bed. I never had the heart to send him back to his room because I knew exactly how he felt. I hated seeing Desiree in the states she ended up in. I'm sure it was worse for him.

It wasn't always bad. Our marriage started out great. I thought she was the one. Third time's a charm, right? Contrary to what a lot of people thought at the time, I didn't just marry her because she was pregnant with Layne. I married her because, at the time, I really did love her. To an extent, I probably always will. Not like I used to. And I never loved her as much as I do Lyric and Mariah, but a part of me really does want her to be happy. Free from whatever haunts her.

I'm not going to lie. Layne's confrontation with her at the courthouse yesterday made me both proud and really fucking sad. Not that he had to confront her in the first place, though that's not something any father wants, but because I let it get that far. I tried over and over again to make things work with her. And I know that if it hadn't been for him, I wouldn't have tried that hard. But I can honestly say I hate myself right now for putting him in a situation where he had to see the shit he saw.

He wasn't wrong. He's seen her come after me. He's seen her throw tantrums. He's seen her hit me. He's seen me block her punches and wrap her in my arms. He's watched as I've sat on the floor with her, cradling her like a child while she screamed about what a horrible husband I was. How having Layne ruined her life. He's seen me yell at her while I dumped wine and tequila down the drain. I was never completely innocent in the fighting and arguing. I never laid a hand on her, but I screamed back more times than I ever should have.

I knew then how much it was affecting Layne. It was hard not to. The older he got, the more he opened up to me about it. And the more he opened up about the effects on him, the more I realized it was over. I couldn't do that to him anymore. The reason I left has always been because of him. Not me or her. It was because Layne was hurting. Our fighting was causing his grades to plummet. He didn't make the team for basketball his eighth grade year because of our fighting. He was so damn tired the day of tryouts, he couldn't do anything right.

I'll never forget him coming home that day and telling me how pissed off he was, words he'd never used before in front of me, because our fighting the couple of nights before had caused him sleepless nights. That he didn't make the team because he kept tripping over his feet and double dribbling. That he forgot how to count and kept getting called for traveling. And how he'd failed a test and a quiz that day because he couldn't concentrate and study.

I sip my coffee, not really comprehending the words on the paper in front of me or the news on the TV. I still don't know everything that happened to her the other night. Matt said he'd talked to her and saw the video feed from the hospital. He told me what he saw; what she said. But I don't have a fucking clue why the hell this all happened in the first place. Do I just take her words at face value? I've never been able to before.

I need the entire story. I was given a cliff notes version because, technically, I'm not supposed to know anything regarding the case, given I'm somewhat involved. I guess there's really no reason why I can't be. It's a question of ethics and integrity for me, though.

"DJ?"

I smile and put my coffee and the paper down on the table as I look up at Lyric, who's adorably rubbing her eyes. "Yeah, baby?"

"What are you doing? It's earlier than you usually get up," she says quietly.

She's right. I haven't even taken a shower or gotten dressed yet. I shut my alarm off before I came out here thirty minutes ago. I didn't sleep a wink last night. After Lyric and Mariah fell asleep, I laid there staring at the ceiling until I finally gave up and decided to just get out of bed. It's barely four in the morning right now.

"Couldn't sleep. That's all. You okay? What are you doing up?"

She sleepily stumbles her way to me, in my t-shirt, and straddles my lap. She wraps her arms around my shoulders and buries her face in my neck. I wrap my arms around her and hug her tightly as I kiss her neck.

"I love Mariah and all her cute noises. But she made a squeaking noise and then talked in her sleep."

I chuckle. "She does that. Rarely. It's only when she's really tired. What did she say?"

"Something about a cute mouse. Mice are not cute. She was cooing."

I can't help but laugh. "Pretty sure Mariah could make anything cute," I rumble against her neck. "Kinda like someone else I know." I grin and let my hands wander down to her perfect ass. "I love that you don't wear panties." I squeeze her ass when I reach it. As usual, she's not wearing panties. She hates wearing them at all, but she never wears them to bed.

She lets out an adorable squeak. I don't need to see her face to know she's blushing. She buries her face in my neck even more, but she presses down on my cock. Which is already hard and waiting for her.

Keeping one hand on her ass, I move the other slowly up her back. When I reach her hair, I tangle my fingers in it and tug lightly. Just enough so she looks at me. I lean in and kiss her. As it always happens, there are explosions behind my eyes as soon as my lips meet hers. She's so soft.

Supple. She tastes so sweet. I never thought I'd be attracted to and want two women as much as I do Lyric and Mariah, but here I am. Head over heels for two incredible women.

My women.

All mine.

I reach down and push my sweats down, not breaking the kiss for even a second. I groan when I slide my dick over her pussy. "Fuck… Already so wet for me," I whisper against her lips.

"I'm always wet for you. For you both. I always want you both. Sometimes, I think you both think I'm too needy. That I'm too much."

I nip her lip and tug her hair lightly as I slowly slide my dick into her tight, wet pussy. "That's the demon talking. What person, male or female, in their right mind would be upset that their girl is always so wet and ready for them?" I thrust into her slowly, holding her tightly to me.

Her pussy pulses around my cock as she meets my thrusts. "Mmm… I don't know…"

"The answer…" I kiss her. I suck lightly on her tongue and nip her lip as I thrust into her. "Is…" I kiss her again and again, thrusting a little faster. She moans and clenches tightly around me. "A person who isn't truly in love." I watch as my words slowly wash over her as I keep thrusting into her.

After a few moments, she smiles and hugs me tighter. "I never thought I'd find anyone who loved me," she whispers.

"Well, now you have two people who truly love you in all of the ways you deserve to be loved."

Lyric shifts and snuggles her face against my neck again. She presses her lips against my skin and breaths with each thrust, but says nothing more. It's all I need from her to know that it's not the fast, hard and deep she usually likes that she needs right now. She doesn't need to be fucked like she usually wants. She needs me to make love to her.

Slow.

So she can feel every thrust. Every ridge. Every kiss. Every touch. Every swipe of my tongue over hers.

So, I give her just that. All of me. I thrust into her deeply and hold her as closely as I can. When I kiss her, I pour every feeling I have for her into it. With each thrust, I pull her into me. I roll my hips against hers so I slide against that sweet little spot inside her that makes her moan.

I feel her start to tremble as she kisses my neck and breathes into me. "DJ…, please…" Her pussy pulses around me. She clenches uncontrollably. I hug her closer and tighter as I thrust.

"Come for me, beautiful girl," I whisper in her ear when I feel her clamp down around my dick.

She hugs me tighter. Her nails dig into my shoulders shakily. She comes hard with small whimpers and soft moans as her hips jerk against mine. "DJ…"

I give her one more hard thrust and bury my cock deep inside her. I come hard for her with a low moan against her neck. "Fuck, Lyric…" I kiss her neck and leave soft kisses across it, up her jaw and cheek, to her lips. I hold her for several minutes as she comes down.

"That felt more intense than any of the other times," she whispers against my neck.

I rub a hand soothingly up and down her back. "You've been struggling these last couple of days. Don't think I haven't felt it. You've been feeling insecure about where you stand in our relationship. That you're being a burden. Everything has been stressful. Mariah has been having a hard time. Even though we talked before the party last night, I know she's still feeling a little anxious. Also, the way her and I got together wasn't how either of us had pictured it. Nor were we expecting the gift we got in you." I kiss her cheek and nuzzle her so she looks at me. I smile at the flush that appears in her cheeks. "These things take time. We continue being open and honest with each other. We take it a day at a time." I kiss her nose and smile lovingly up at her. "We fight through it. You. Me. Mariah. Together."

She nods with a soft smile. "Together."

"Forever." I grin.

"Forever and always." Her smile brightens at the use of the slogan we've created for our relationship.

Forever and always.

"That's my girl." I wrap her tighter in my arms as I shift us and stand. "I'm going to shower and get dressed. You, beautiful, are going to snuggle with our girl and get more sleep."

She wraps her legs around my waist and arms tighter around my shoulders. "Yes, sir."

"Good girl." I kiss her softly as I walk to our room. I glance at Layne's open door and smile. "I'm grateful he's with Beckett. I love my son, but that would have been awkward if he came out to me fucking you."

She giggles and blushes. "Traumatizing for a child."

I kiss her again. "He'd never get over it." I carry her to our bed and lay her down next to Mariah. She looks up at me through her lashes and cuddles our girl. "Such a sexy sight. I love seeing you two together."

Lyric blushes darker and hides in Mariah's hair. I pull the blankets up higher over them and tuck it tight around them before I head for the shower. By the time I'm done, Lyric is fast asleep and curled up in Mariah's arms. I smile and contemplate crawling into bed with them, but I know I have a long day ahead of me. One where I'll be getting the truth behind what happened and putting Desiree behind me and my family forever.

✯✯✯

I rub a hand down my face. "Not that I don't trust you, Matt. I just need to see it for myself."

"It's fucked up, DJ. Really. But if that's what you want, it's loaded up for you. I had a feeling you'd ask." Matt looks at his watch. "I have a lunch date with Luca." He taps a couple of keys on his keyboard. "Everything is up for you. Reports. The video. Hospital surveillance. Interviews. I know you have your issues with Desiree, but she was telling the truth this time."

I sigh as I watch him stand. He gives my shoulder a squeeze on his way out. He closes the door behind him. It takes me a few more moments after he leaves to actually move, but I finally do. I sit down in his chair and watch the video she shot first.

Like Matt said, it starts out with everyone snorting a line. It's one of the charges brought against the Sergeant and the two officers in the video. Doing drugs isn't a good thing in any circumstance, but doing them while on shift is a whole other ballgame. They add drinking to the mix. The next thing happening is the group sex.

I skip a lot of it until the Sergeant's hand comes over the camera. I pull it back a little and turn the audio up. That was odd and something Matt

134

didn't say. He told me the video had been stopped, but didn't mention that it was before any of the roughness started.

"We won't be needing this anymore," he says.

"Wait, what?" Desiree says in the background as the Sergeant's hand comes down over the camera filming him. .

I furrow my eyebrows as it cuts to another angle. "Fucking hell," I whisper.

I watch as Desiree watches him crush the camera. Not that there was a point in that shit. He should know crushing the camera isn't going to stop us from getting the feed if it's being uploaded in real time. If he wanted to keep things quiet, he should have made her show him that it wasn't being automatically uploaded to something somewhere.

He then stalks towards her. I'll hand it to her. She's smarter than she looks. Filming her encounters, and then using another camera just in case that one goes out. Or to protect herself in cases like this. It's intelligent.

Desiree is clearly freaked out as she watches him. The other two hold her down as the Sergeant cuffs her. The next thirty minutes makes me physically ill. They not only take turns with her, very roughly, as she screams, but she says repeatedly that she doesn't want to do it anymore. Every time she protests, she's slapped so hard, I'm sure she blacks out for a few seconds. She fights and screams until she can't anymore.

And even then, they don't stop.

I shut the video off because if I don't, I'm going to lose the contents of my stomach. And since I've been so fucking nervous about watching this and finding out the damn truth, I haven't eaten much. Anything that comes out of me would be nothing but bile.

"Fuck me," I mumble.

I move onto the hospital surveillance and watch as both officers clearly drive her to the entrance of the ER and push her out. They stay there for a few moments. I agree with Matt. I think they're blaring their horn. When a nurse starts running out the doors, they take off like a bat out of hell.

I barely look up when Matt comes back into his office. He says nothing and closes the door behind him. He takes the seat I had been sitting in before I moved and watches me as I pour through everything he has. The confessions of the cops. They corroborated everything both videos show.

Desiree's statement. Everything she told Matt after he got her to admit the truth is everything I just saw on the video.

On a whim, I print out the written confessions of all the cops and Desiree. When I'm finished, I take them off the printer and stack them neatly in front of me as Matt hands me an empty folder. I put them into it.

"When you show her, DJ, remember what she's told you about her past," Matt says quietly.

"I know."

Lyric was assaulted by her ex. It was the only relationship she's ever been in. She was with two other people after that, and they both left her after getting what they wanted from her. Sex. It's always just been about sex. When they got it, they were done with her. And, in the case of her first relationship, if he didn't, she got a beating. The word 'no' was met with an even more vicious beating and him taking what he wanted regardless of her cries. She learned early on to give him anything he asked for.

When Matt told me at the party last night that Lyric hadn't been sleeping, it confirmed my suspicions. I had a feeling she was having a hard time with this because of where she came from. She doesn't believe Desiree because of all she did to me and Layne.

But she's also struggling because she feels that Desiree is going to keep hurting us. That she's lying about all of this and manipulating us. She feels like it's only a matter of time before she comes back to hurt us.

It's what happened to her. She believed her ex when he told her he was done. When she was moving on from what happened, he would come back and hurt her again. It was a vicious cycle that went on for years. Lyric has a difficult time trusting anyone like Desiree now because of it. Even if she's not lying about it all, what if she's using it for her own gain? Either way, Lyric is terrified that our family still isn't safe.

Mariah, on the other hand, is on the opposite end of the spectrum. She was also a survivor of abuse. She saw something different in Desiree than what Lyric saw. It's one of the reasons she went so quiet. She didn't want to upset anyone by telling either of us that she didn't agree. That while she was proud of Layne for telling Desiree off and was all for her not being in our lives, she could also see the hurt and pain and regret that Lyric didn't see. That I'm honestly not sure if I did. Though, even if Lyric did see it, I don't think she would fully believe it. I probably wouldn't either.

Which is why I'm showing them both these statements. I don't know if it will do anything in bringing them a little closer together on this. I don't even know if it will help either of them. But I do know that they both need to see it, and we need to talk about it because, like I told Lyric this morning, we're going to get through all of this together.

Forever and always.

Chapter Fourteen

☆ Mariah ☆

(Six Months Later)

"Thank you," I say softly with a tired smile as I hand the young woman in front of me her signed book. "Don't forget to grab your bag of goodies."

I smile brighter as she clutches the book to her chest and nods. She scurries happily to the door where there are people handing out customized tote bags filled with swag to everyone leaving. No one knows that my entire revamped first series is included in there. I'm handing out the first revamped book and custom signing them all, but all of the others in the series have been signed and are included in the goodies. Along with bookmarks, water bottles, mugs, stickers, pens and pencils. Even keychains.

"Not too much longer," Luca says from behind me. He squeezes my shoulder soothingly.

"I don't think you realize how calming that is," I say as I look up at him.

He shrugs and winks. "I may have had help."

I chuckle. I know he did. I've been doing a lot of book signings lately. Usually Lyric and DJ are with me, but not today. Lyric had something to do. Something she's being very secretive about. Every time it's brought up, she giggles like a schoolgirl and just says that we'll have to wait and see what's happening. It's beyond adorable.

DJ has been working on a time consuming case that's not only had him going into work early most mornings, but is also keeping him at work later than usual. It hasn't stopped him from making us both fall more and more in love with him, though. On the nights he stays later, he always surprises us with takeout. And if he goes in early, he never fails to leave us notes telling us how much he loves us.

Lyric and I both work diligently together to make sure that he has a healthy lunch to take with him. And that there's something for breakfast already ready to go for him so he doesn't have to spend much time on it. Or so he doesn't just stop and get a donut and coffee on his way in. He's been known to do that, but it's not enough to keep him going through the morning, no matter what he says. He gets far more testy at the department, and Lyric and I always get a phone call from Matt telling us to tell him to quit being an asshole.

It's a joke between us all. Something that makes us all feel closer. It's something Lyric and I have never had. Most of our lives have been spent with one or two people in our lives that we honestly felt like we could trust and were comfortable with.

Lyric and I have been spending most of our days together. My lease on my apartment was up a couple of months ago. I never renewed it because I was never in my apartment. I'd moved most of my things into DJ's. When my lease expired, all I really wanted for furniture was my chair. Lyric fell in love with the matching one, so she begged me to take that one as well. Everything else was donated to the Salvation Army.

Lyric has been finding her footing in the relationship. She's feeling far less vulnerable and much more confident. She's finally starting to understand that she's just as much a part of us as DJ and I are. As soon as she realized that, it's like the floodgates opened. We all became so close and opened up so much to our relationship. And now, well, it's like we've been together our whole lives. Everything comes so naturally to us. There's no fear. No hesitation. There's nothing but us.

It feels amazing. Being in a relationship filled with love and trust. It's unlike anything any of us have ever felt before. I wasn't positive a love like this existed. A love like what I write about in my books had always been fantasy. The fact that I found it and am living it makes me feel whole. Complete.

"I want to be a writer because of you," a guy who I'd say might still be in college says to me. "I get razzed because of it, but fuck. Your books are amazing."

My eyes widen at the fact that it's a guy. "Wow. Thank you. What's your name?"

"Parker."

I start signing his book. "Parker. That's a really huge compliment. Thank you. How did you hear about my work?"

He grins. "My sister. I was bored as hell one night. She fell asleep with one of your books. I decided to see what her obsession with you was. I was hooked. I bought all your books the next day. I have a bookshelf in my bedroom dedicated to you. I always thought the covers weren't nearly as good as the writer. Didn't tell the story."

I hand him the book with a nod. "I've heard that before. It's why I had them redone. I didn't want them to look like an amateur did them. I hired a very talented designer. Hopefully, everyone likes them as much as I do."

He takes the book with a huge grin. "I know I do. Much better." Parker looks at Luca. "Uh… Maybe I could get a picture?" He looks down at me hopefully.

I smile. "Sure. I don't, usually, because then everyone will want one, but if you want to hang out a bit? We could discuss your writing a little. I have my own publishing company, so if you're serious, I'd love to help you out."

"Holy shit, yes. No question." Parker's eyes light up. "I'd be insane to pass up a deal like that."

"Perfect. Um…" I look up at Luca.

Catching onto what I need from him immediately, he points to the door. "You can hang out over there. There's a chair behind the table. Just tell them I sent you over there."

Parker nods and scurries over to the door. He has a quick conversation with one of the people who's handing out the bags. After confirming with Luca via a head nod, Parker parks himself in the chair behind the table.

I giggle when he starts putting one of each thing from the piles on the table into the tote bags. "Looks like they put him to work with the swag."

Luca chuckles as I finish signing the last few books people give to me when they come up to my table. Luca is acting as my security today. He's done it for every single book signing I've had since not long after I met him. He doesn't need to, but he says he does it because he likes to.

When he learned that my previous security had let me get bombarded with fans who pushed and shoved at me, he was furious. He immediately took control. He fired the security company and, with Matt and DJ's help, started his own security firm. He hired a couple of men that they all trusted to work with him.

Luca's business was almost immediately thriving. Now, he's one of the largest security firms in Gainesville. But he never forgot why he started the firm. He assigned himself as my personal security and has been with me ever since. I don't know what I would do without him now. Thank all of the Gods he has his own security firm and can handle everything I need him to.

When they were setting this all in motion, DJ had told him about my anxiety and how to help me if I get too nervous. DJ has almost always been at my signings, but on the rare occasions he isn't, Luca does very well at helping me when I need him to.

"That was the last one, Rih," Luca says.

"Thankfully. Fighting anxiety to do my duty is hard." I give him a half teasing, half serious smile. I like having contact with my fans, but it's exhausting because I struggle so hard being away from the safety of home.

"I know." He hugs me. I melt against him.

"In case I never told you, thank you. For everything. You didn't have to do this."

"As I always tell you, I want to."

"I think I understand more now. Now that DJ and Lyric and I are together. You saw her in me. Protective brother instincts and all that."

He chuckles, and it rumbles through me, grounding me even more. He's so steady. Safe. Like DJ and Lyric and Matt are. I'm so glad I know him. "Sure. Protective brother. Let's go with that. And not that your boyfriend threatens my life daily if I let anything happen to either of his girls or his son. I think the asshole forgets one of his girls is my sister. She was mine first."

I laugh. "That is not true." My eyes widen, and I look up at him. "Is that true?"

He grins. "Maybe." He shrugs. "Maybe not."

I swat him teasingly. "You seriously fit right into my fucked up circle of trusted souls. You're as much of an asshole as DJ and Matt are." I push him away with a giggle.

He puts a hand up to his heart and feigns shock. "I am not *an* asshole," he says in an exaggerated British accent that he doesn't need because he literally is British. "I am *the* asshole."

I laugh again as he guides me over to where Parker is sitting. "How'd tote bag stuffing go?" I ask with a smile.

He grins. "It was boring as hell, but holy shit, Mariah. You have a lot of cool swag! A bookmark customized to each book. A series notebook. Pens and pencils for each book. A keychain for each book. The tote bag is customized to the series. And then you even include the rest of the books in the series! All autographed!"

"One day, I'm going to figure out how to customize all of the autographs. But signing nine books for one hundred people would have likely killed me. My hand would have fallen off. Maybe I'll get names of all the people who buy the tickets to get in. Then customize each prize bag for each of them. I could take several days to do that before events like this."

"That would be amazing," Parker says.

"So, Parker. What do you plan on writing? What genre?" I ask him.

"Romance, for sure. There aren't a lot of male romance authors out there. I think it would be a good idea to write it from a male's perspective. I think you, for example, get the male perspective down really well. But there are a lot of authors who definitely don't. I've also seen a couple male authors who can't get the female perspective down. I wrote a manuscript. I had males and females look at it and tell me they think I got it right. I'd be honored if you'd take a look."

"I'd love to. I doubt you brought it with you, so maybe email me a copy?"

"Yeah, for sure."

I hand him my card and take the picture with him that I promised I would. After he happily leaves, Luca helps me pack everything up, though, it's not much since I handed everything out to the fans who showed up for the signing.

When we're done, I yawn. "I'm totally ready to go home."

"You look pretty beat."

I yawn again. "I'm looking forward to a nap on my girl's lap while we wait for our man."

Luca laughs as we walk out to his car. "Well, your girl has plans. Big ones. And your man is on his way home. Matt just texted a little bit ago and asked how close we were to being done."

I raise an eyebrow as we get into his car. "Why do I feel like you all are conspiring against me?"

Luca gives me his trademark cocky as crap grin. "Because we all are."

I giggle. "Okay. What is Lyric planning? Spill."

"Not a chance. Blood runs deep. I'm loyal to my sister."

I laugh. "You just don't want to face her fury. You know she's dangerous when she's angry."

"Hey. You've never seen her. She once broke a glass on the counter when she squeezed it as she was glaring at me, and didn't flinch as she bled from the cut."

"I call bullshit to the infinite degree. Lyric cannot stand pain. She would have been screaming in agony."

"No shit. She kept the glare up until I apologized. Then she started crying. Well, screaming. She started screaming from the pain." He chuckles and shakes his head. He pauses before he continues. "It was when she saw the state the kitchen was in after we bandaged her up that she panicked. She rushed over and tried to help clean while apologizing over and over. She didn't seem to hear us when we told her it was okay and tried to get her to stop. Matt ended up carrying her into the den, and we both helped to calm her. She fell asleep on his lap. I went back and cleaned up the kitchen while she slept." He shakes his head again like he's ridding himself of the memory.

I know he is thinking about what she has told him about her relationship. I know he still feels guilty that he didn't see it. That he wasn't

143

able to stop it before she got hurt. I know Matt feels the same way. Lyric is his little sister. Their little sister.

"I never knew that," I say softly. I know Lyric has had to fight to become the incredible woman she is today, but I hate that she was ever made to feel like that. Like she had to clean up a mess while she was hurt.

He glances over at me as we pull up outside my apartment. "I look at her now, and I'm in awe of her strength. Of how far she has come. And I have you and DJ to thank for that. Oh, I know Matt and I had a large part in how she has grown, but you both have embraced her for who she is and let her shine."

I smile as we get out of the car. He takes the box from the backseat and carries it with him as he follows me inside. "Lyric is one of the two best things that have ever happened to me. I know she doesn't know it, or maybe doesn't understand it, but she saved me as much as I did her. Her and DJ are everything to me. I could give up writing right now, in this moment, and still be happy because I have them."

We step into the elevator. I smile softly and fall quiet. Lyric and DJ really are everything to me. I wonder every single day where I would be without them. I can't even imagine my life anymore without them both in it. They've become such a huge part of me that being without them would be like a part of my soul was gone. I don't think I'd survive it. I know I wouldn't.

I stifle a yawn as we step off the elevator and see DJ squatting in front of our door with his back against the wall opposite of it. I raise an eyebrow in confusion. He's still wearing the black slacks he went to work in and his shoulder holster over his dress shirt. The bag he carries all of his gear in, like his gym clothes and all of his police equipment, is sitting next to him. His sunglasses are perched on his head.

"What... are... you doing...?" I ask, bewildered, as I look down at him.

He looks up at me. "Your guess is as good as mine, baby girl." He looks back at the door. "I came home. Matt was with me. I opened the door. Lyric squeaked and launched at the door. She pulled Matt inside and told me I'm not allowed in there yet. To give her five minutes." He looks at his watch. "That was four minutes and seven seconds ago."

I blink, then crack up. "You are not timing it."

He grins and looks up at me again as he holds up his wrist. "Timing it." His watch is counting down.

"You know she'll be longer than five minutes, just to be a brat now because you timed her." I laugh again.

He winks at me. "I'm counting on it."

I bite my lip and make a show of crossing my legs. "Why does that make me all wet?" I whisper.

"Fuck. Shut up." Luca covers his ears. "La! La! La! La! La!"

DJ laughs. "So, that's where she gets that from," he says, referring to Lyric's covering her ears when she doesn't want to hear something embarrassing. He stands and wraps both arms around me. He kisses me so deeply that my head spins and I forget my name. For a brief moment, I'm fairly certain I'm floating. When he pulls away, he's wearing a sexy grin. "Hi."

"Hi," I whisper.

"Missed you."

"Missed you, too."

"How did the signing go? I'm sorry I couldn't be there."

"It went okay. Depending on how good his book is, I might be signing my first male romance author. I can't wait to tell Lyric. She's been looking for a good one. He's going to email me his manuscript. I'm hoping Lyric will read it with me."

"I'm positive she'd love to." He runs his fingers through my hair.

"How did your day go? Any breaks in that case?"

"Solved it, actually. Made the arrest earlier. Lyric is going to be really excited about that. I also have another surprise for you both."

"Oh?"

"Yep. But I want to tell you at the same time. Well, show you."

I let out a happy squeal and hug him tighter. "Whatever it is, I can't wait!"

Suddenly, the door to the apartment swings open. I turn to see Layne grinning as he follows a beaming Matt out of the apartment. Layne drops a kiss to my head as Matt winks and leads both him and Luca down the hall.

"Have fun, mom and dad!" Layne calls over his shoulder.

DJ chuckles and shakes his head. He takes my hand and leads me to the door after he slings his bag over his shoulder. He squeezes my hand

and knocks lightly with a huge smile. I giggle and bounce on my toes. I don't know what's happening, but I love all of it.

"You can come in!" Lyric calls. "But you have to close your eyes!"

I giggle as DJ closes his eyes. I close mine and let him lead me into the house. I hear him close the door behind us and Lyric giggling. I feel her soft hands take ours and lead us further into the room.

"You're adorable. Can we open our eyes?" DJ asks.

"Nope! Keep walking with me," Lyric says happily.

"You're guiding us to the bedroom," DJ says, matter-of-factly.

Lyric giggles. "Shh." After a few more moments, she stops. "Okay. Get changed into something comfy. Then come back out."

"With our eyes closed?" DJ teases.

"No, silly! You can open your eyes. Just don't take forever."

"Got it. No taking forever," I say as seriously as possible, trying to fight back a grin. Lyric giggles as she closes the door behind us.

DJ laughs. "She didn't give us the choice of what to wear." He nods towards the bed.

I laugh when I see my favorite t-shirt of DJ's and a pair of tiny pink shorts. "I can't help but notice that she left you a pair of gray sweats and no shirt."

"She must know I'm hot," DJ says with a grin as he starts to put his stuff away and change.

"Oh, you're hot alright."

DJ swats my ass with a grin. "So are you."

After quickly changing into Lyric's chosen outfits, DJ and I make our way out to the living room. I've been smelling something delectable, but I can't quite place what it is. It takes a back seat to the sight in front of us, though.

Set up at the table between the kitchen and living room is dinner, but all the platters are covered, so I can't see what it is. There aren't any lights on at all in the entire room, but Lyric has several fake candles that look totally real lit and strategically placed throughout the room to give it the softest, most beautiful glow. She knows fire scares me. Even candles. Though, I make an exception sometimes when I really, really, really want to smell my sugar cookie candle. I can't have it near me, though. The flame freaks me out.

"Oh my God," I whisper.

In the middle of the table is one large candle that gives the illusion of a flickering flame. It's placed in the middle of a bouquet of dark pink carnations, my favorite flower, black roses, DJ's favorite flower, and purple lilies Lyric's favorite flower. Surrounding the bouquet are small tea lights.

"Jesus, baby," DJ says softly.

The couch holds our favorite fleece blanket to spread across us all and snuggle in. On the coffee table is *The Day After Tomorrow*, my favorite movie, *Hours*, Lyric's favorite movie, and *Deadpool*, DJ's favorite movie.

But in the center of it all is Lyric. Her hands are clasped together in front of her. She's wearing her favorite t-shirt of DJ's and a pair of purple shorts that are exactly like the ones she chose for me. She's looking at us both through her eyelashes so submissively and hopeful, that my heart physically aches at the amount of love I feel for her.

"I made steak and chicken burritos," she says softly. Her eyes meet mine. "Yours has steak, chicken, sour cream, tri-blend cheese, black olives, and tomatoes." She blushes when I smile brightly. She looks up at DJ. "And yours has steak, chicken, chipotle ranch, tomatoes, green peppers, red peppers, and pepperjack cheese."

DJ grins. "You know us very well. That's our favorite Mexican food."

She smiles brightly at the praise and hurries to the table. "I also made Spanish rice and refried beans. And I looked up how to make homemade crisps and salsa. I made Matt taste everything, and he loved it. And for dessert…" She looks up at us both as we sit down. She sits down after we do. "I made peach cobbler with a scoop of your favorite ice cream."

"You're just going all out, aren't you?" DJ leans over and kisses her softly.

I look at her hopefully. "Cake Batter ice cream?"

She nods when DJ pulls away. I squeak and lean in. I kiss her as I bounce in my chair happily. "And Rocky Road for DJ," she says when I pull away.

I'm so excited for all of this that I nearly forget to tell her about what happened today. I'm only reminded when DJ starts telling her about his day. I wait for him to finish before I tell her my news and am elated when she squeals in excitement and tells me she'd love to read his manuscript with me.

A person would think that our girlfriend's beauty and sweetness would be the highlight of my day. Of anyone's day. But as we all finish what I'm pretty convinced is the best burritos, peach cobbler, and ice cream I've ever had, we all cuddle on the couch to watch movies. Before Lyric has a chance to push play, though, DJ has to go and cement this as one of the best days of my life.

Saying nothing, he pulls out a folder as he sits down and sets five images of gorgeous houses on the table. Lyric and I both look at each other in confusion before our bewildered gazes turn to him. He's grinning as he leans back.

"Okay... You've got us intrigued," I say.

"What is it?" Lyric asks.

"Houses," DJ answers. The smile doesn't leave his lips as he watches us with his hands folded behind his head. Lyric and I share another baffled look.

"Okay... Why are you showing us houses?" Lyric asks.

"Well," DJ begins. He leans forward and rests his elbows on his knees as he looks at me. "After I left Desiree, I could have gotten my own place. But with the divorce up in the air, I didn't want to end up giving her two houses. I didn't know which way my hearing was going to go. Judges are people, too. For all I knew, my judge could have sided with Desiree just because. It's why I chose an apartment. I figured I'd live here until my divorce was finalized. Then, I'd get my own place for me and Layne. But things changed."

I blush, then blush again when I see Lyric's pretty pink coloring. "Us," I whisper.

"Yes. Truth be told, before Lyric, I didn't see myself leaving here. I had no intention of starting a relationship with you," he says as he looks at me. "You know I wasn't looking for a relationship and didn't want to ruin our friendship by diving into this. I didn't want wife number four. No matter who she was. I wasn't going to get married again. But I also liked being around you. Layne liked having you around. I was making plans to just stay here for good. It's a good neighborhood. Good place to live.

You're comfortable here. It's not far away from HQ. It's secure. Lots of advantages, but it mostly came back to you."

I hug his arm and hide with a shy smile. "I got pretty used to you being around."

He kisses the top of my head before turning to Lyric. "And then we met you. After Mariah and I got together, I'd been playing with the idea of asking Mariah to move into a house with me, but when you came into our lives, I decided that while this place is cozy, you both need a place you can truly relax. Somewhere that we can start fresh and make our own memories. The never getting married again idea was thrown out as soon as I kissed Mariah. But it was cemented when we met you. But we all need a place we can truly call ours."

"So, you chose five houses," Lyric says with a soft chuckle.

DJ grins. "I did."

He starts the movie and picks up each of the pictures with information and prices on the houses. He pulls us both back and settles us into him. As the movie begins, we all look at the houses and talk about each of them, and as the night goes on, I feel lighter and lighter.

Like I'm finally starting my life.

Like it's been waiting for this moment to begin.

Like I had to find the loves of my life before I could truly feel whole.

Epilogue

☆ Lyric ☆

(Three Months Later)

"Can we take them off now?" I ask, bouncing on my toes.

"No," DJ responds. "Not yet."

I squeeze Mariah's hand. We're both barely containing our excitement. DJ has had us blindfolded since we left our apartment. Layne keeps laughing when one of us lets out a squeak that we can't keep in any longer.

"How come he doesn't have to be blindfolded?" Mariah asks. I know she's pouting. I don't need to see it. I can hear it in her voice. She's so pretty when she pouts.

DJ laughs. "Because he's in on the entire scheme against you both. He doesn't need one."

It's my turn to pout. "I call a flag."

Layne cracks up. "It's a penalty, mom. You throw a flag."

"Yeah," I say as seriously as possible. "And the flag is thrown for the penalty. So, I call a flag. I will die on this hill."

Mariah giggles. "Adorable."

"American football is ridiculously confusing anyway. It's not football."

DJ laughs. "Really? This is why you throw M&M's at the TV when something bad happens? Because American football is ridiculously confusing? You know more than you let on. And you like it more than you want us to believe, too." He taps my ass as he stops us both from walking.

Mariah and I are vibrating with energy. Neither of us like surprises at all, but when DJ or Layne are involved, we've both decided we're huge fans. I suddenly feel Layne take my hands, gently making me release Mariah's hand. I know it's him because DJ is still behind me. Layne leads me by both my hands somewhere, but I don't know where. Inside somewhere, maybe? The ground feels different underneath me.

As I try to figure it out, I feel Mariah next to me again. As if she's the magnet for my soul, my hand automatically finds hers. We grasp each other again. I can feel the energy she's feeling zipping through my arm like an electric current. I'm sure she feels exactly the same thing from me.

"Okay. Ready?" DJ asks. I feel his fingers on the back of my head where the blindfold is tied.

"Ready!" I say enthusiastically.

"So ready!" Mariah exclaims.

DJ undoes the blindfold as Mariah and I hold each other's hand. I blink a few times as the blindfold is pulled away.

"Surprise!" a few other voices yell from in front of us. It takes me a few moments to realize it's Matt, Beckett, and Luca.

And we're in a house.

One I recognize, I think.

I look at Mariah, who's blinking adorably at our surroundings. DJ and Layne are standing side by side with matching stances and grins and their arms folded across their chests. Matt, Beckett, and Luca are all grinning from ear to ear as Mariah and I try to get our bearings.

"Oh… my… God…," Mariah says with wide eyes. "DJ, is this the house? The one we picked?"

DJ grins and nods. "Layne and I have been over here every chance we could get to decorate it and get the furniture in. There weren't a lot of repairs to be done. They've all been taken care of already."

My eyes fill with tears as I look around with a soft smile. "It's… perfect… It's so perfect."

"It's beautiful…," Mariah whispers.

The house is fully furnished. I can see pots and pans in the kitchen, which makes me think there are dishes and everything in the cabinets. All things DJ sneakily had us pick out online. I'd call him a sneak, but I'm too busy admiring the house in awe.

The walls have been painted a warm and relaxing beige. The furniture is black. The carpet is a gorgeous beige to match the walls. Mariah pulls me around the house as we both take everything in. There's a gym in the basement with a game room across from it. There's even a small little kitchen with a portable fridge, and a small bathroom.

DJ is always prepared for everything. He's made it into our storm room. I don't even need to ask him. In a closet that's built into the wall are several bags. They're all filled with things like protein bars and anything else he thinks we'll need in the event we end up down here for a couple of days. I'm sure there are the same types of bags in the bedrooms upstairs. DJ even has blankets down here and air mattresses.

Mariah leads me upstairs. DJ, Layne, Matt, Luca, and Beckett are all watching us with giant grins as we fly up the stairs, giggling. Our bedroom has a large, California King sized bed. The bathroom is the largest bathroom I've ever seen, complete with a jacuzzi tub and walk-in shower that makes me blush. It's large enough for the three of us to not only fit, but move around in. It's perfect for Mariah, who can only take showers with me or DJ. It's a way we've discovered we can get around her panic.

"I'm in love. I want to marry the bathroom," Mariah says as she stares at it.

I giggle. "Too bad you're already in a committed relationship." I tug her hand and pull her back down the stairs with me. I tilt my head. "Though, I'm pretty in love with that walk-in closet. I might marry it."

DJ and Mariah both let out possessive growls as we reach the bottom of the stairs. "Not a chance in hell, sexy girl." DJ's lips crash to mine.

I squeak and melt into him. I barely have a second to catch my breath when he pulls away before Mariah is kissing me like I'm her favorite ice cream. I melt into her as she tangles her fingers in my hair. DJ's hand finds my butt. Just as Mariah pulls away, he slaps it, making me jump and moan at the same time.

"Ours," Mariah rumbles against my ear as she whispers in it.

"And don't you forget that," DJ says low and growly.

"Would you both stop mauling my baby sister in front of me? Geez…," Luca grumbles with a laugh. I look over at him and giggle when I see his face is buried in Matt's chest.

DJ laughs. "Okay, okay." He takes my hand and Mariah's. "One last thing before we go outside." He leads us down a hallway to a room at the back of the house. He turns, drops Mariah's hand with a wink, and reaches behind him to open the door. He flicks on a light, then takes Mariah's hand again. Walking backwards, he leads us into a den with a giant seventy inch TV mounted to the wall. "Tahdah," he sing-songs.

"Oh, wow," Mariah whispers.

Like the rest of the house, this room is filled with warm colors. The walls, carpet, and furniture match the decor throughout the house. Even the light coming from the ceiling fan above us is calming and relaxing. There's a floor to ceiling window with a sliding glass door leading to the backyard, but I notice the black blackout curtains. While they are currently open, they can be closed. I know DJ did it this way for me and Mariah. This is our safe place.

And I feel it. The entire house feels new and inviting. Ours. But this room… This room feels like family. It feels like us. It's filled with love. I can feel it flowing through me. It's perfect. So perfect, in fact, that with our loved ones surrounding us, I make a decision.

It's time.

I take a deep, steadying breath, and set out to do something I never thought I'd do.

I look at Luca. He grins widely and hands me three large containers. Kind of like those ones you get in those claw machines, only a little bigger. They have to be in order to hold the small boxes inside them. One of them is pink. The other is green. The last is red. DJ and Layne are just as confused as Mariah, but Matt, Luca, and Beckett are all in on this. I'd planned on doing it at a barbecue tonight at Matt and Luca's. It's why Luca has them. But this… It's perfect.

Everything about this moment is perfect.

I hand Mariah the pink one, DJ the green one, and Layne the red one. I take another breath. "I never believed I would be standing here with you. For years, I thought I would be alone. Before Luca moved us here, I was in a very dark place. It pains me to say that I wouldn't be here today if it wasn't for him. I thought when he first left, that was it. He would live his life in the States, and I would continue to drown in the UK. I was spiraling. I barely ate or slept. I thought I was hiding it well. I mean, none of my family noticed. So, I didn't believe Luca would either."

Mariah sniffles. "Oh, my love," she whispers.

I continue on, bravery filling me more and more the longer I speak. "Luca came home for the first time a few months later. He looked happier than I had ever seen him. He told me that he had found his home, but he'd also found something he never thought he would. He found Matt. He told me about the moment Matt pulled him over, about their first date, and about Matt helping him find his place. I was happy for him. If anyone deserved to find their forever, it was my brother. But I also felt envious. There he was… happy and, even if he wouldn't admit it at the time, in love. I was still stuck living with our mother and sinking deeper and deeper into my dark pit."

"Baby…," DJ whispers. This is all stuff I haven't quite told them. Mariah opened up and told me all about her past. Her ex. Being sexually assaulted when she was seven. All of it. Even DJ told me his story. But this… I haven't been brave enough.

But I am today.

"I'm ashamed to admit that I ran from him that day. He left me alone for about an hour before he burst into my room, threw me over his shoulder and took me back to his hotel with him. He sat me down, made me my favorite hot cocoa, and confronted me about everything I hadn't told him. He could see even through our video chats how much weight I had lost. How the shadows in my eyes had gotten darker. That I wasn't living. Just… existing. And he refused to let it happen any more. I broke down. I told him everything. How I couldn't keep going much longer. I felt dead inside."

I can tell Mariah wants to throw her arms around me, but DJ pulls her into his side instead. I'm so grateful to him for being able to read me like that because if she hugged me, I'd break down and not be able to continue.

I take another breath. "After hugging me for what felt like hours until I had calmed down, Luca told me that he had already set the wheels in motion. He told me that he had applied for a Visa for me. That Matt was going to sponsor me. He told me that as soon as dad finished packing my things and brought my suitcases over to the hotel, we would be booking our flight back to Gainesville. Within a few hours, we were at the airport and flying home. I didn't leave the house for at least a month. I barely even let myself meet Matt, and later, Beckett. But slowly, I started to trust them. I was able to be around them for longer periods. I started to feel like me again."

"I'm so proud of you," Luca whispers. I don't think he meant for me to hear it, but I do.

"It's funny, but on those game nights? When you and Mariah and some others would come over? Beckett would always try to convince me to come out. That his Uncle DJ and Aunt Mariah were awesome. That you wouldn't care if I sat silently in the corner. But I couldn't do it. What none of them know is that I did come out, though not far enough to see anyone or be seen. I would sit at the top of the stairs and listen to you all. To the games. I just couldn't go any further, no matter how many times I tried to give myself pep talks."

I shake my head realizing I've gone a bit off topic.

"Sorry... I never thought I would have a love like Matt and Luca found in each other. A love where I was accepted for who I am. Where I was able to be myself without fear of being belittled or beaten. Sure, I had Luca, and then Matt and Beckett, but that's different. That's family love. That's not the kind of love that you find in the heart that's made for you. Then I met Mariah. And I felt something in me stir. A kind of flame that filled me with warmth. An intense need that made me want to curl into it. I think I started to fall for you then. I didn't want to ruin one of the most important relationships I had had outside of my little family, so I pushed it away. And then I saw you, DJ, and it was like that small flame burst into an inferno. I could feel a connection sizzling between us. And even though it terrified me, I yearned for it. I didn't know what it meant at the time, but I wanted to curl up in your lap and never leave. And while the dominant in you called to my submissive side, it was your heart that made me fall for you even more than I already had in that one glance. I was terrified the day you both approached me, but I also had never felt safer."

I take another breath.

"I have never felt the kind of love and acceptance I have felt when I'm with you. I don't just have the love of my partners, but I also have the love of our son, something I never thought I would have. If you asked me whether I would change where I started, what I have been through in my life, I would say no. Because it led me here. To you. It led me to my forever."

I chuckle a little and wipe my eyes. I know I'm crying, but I can't stop the tears.

"God, I'm a mess. What I'm trying to say is that I love you both with all I am." I look away from DJ and Mariah to Layne. "I love you, Layne. Thank you for giving me the honor of being your mom." I take another deep breath. "In those balls is a symbol of my commitment to you. As your mom," I smile softly at Layne, then turn my attention back to Mariah and DJ. "As your partner. I want forever with you. This is my way of asking if you'll be my forever, too."

DJ, taking my hint, looks down at the ball in his hand and opens it. Mariah and Layne both follow his lead. Things have been going very well for me with my cover business. I've gotten a lot of new clients through Mariah's company. Which is how I could afford to buy each of the things I did without putting myself in debt.

Mariah gasps when she sees the black velvet box inside the ball. She quickly opens it and puts on a ring that matches mine, which I carefully pull from my jeans pocket and slide onto my finger. It's a white-gold band with a blue diamond in the middle. On one side of it is a smaller pink diamond. On the other is a smaller purple diamond that matches the size of the pink one. And on each side of them is an even smaller red diamond. I had the rings specially designed to include all of us and our favorite colors. DJ's, being blue, is in the middle. Mariah and I are on each side of him. And Layne surrounds us all. Like he's the glue that holds everyone together.

DJ grins when he pulls his ring out. Like ours, the band is white-gold. There are small diamonds in his ring that are in the same order as ours. The only difference is that they're much smaller and are snuggled down inside the center of his ring.

Layne watches Mariah and DJ put their rings on their fingers. They have huge smiles that make my heart melt. I want to hug them, but I'm rooted to my spot, waiting for Layne. When he finally opens his, I hold my breath. His ring is the same as DJ's. It's just on a sterling silver chain that he can wear around his neck.

No one says a single word. I watch Layne put the chain around his neck, and then they all three glomp me. They hug me so close and tight. Mariah and DJ kiss my lips, cheeks, and neck. Layne stays snuggled at my back, and for the first time in my life I feel… complete.

★★★

Several hours later, after Matt and Luca leave, taking Beckett and Layne with them, I collapse on the brand new and incredibly soft bed. DJ said it's breathable. I don't know exactly what that means, but I think it has something to do with the fact that it always stays cool or something.

"I love this house," I say. "I love both of you. I love that it's next door to Matt and Luca. I don't know how we got so lucky that this house opened up."

"It was definitely a no-brainer when you saw the address," DJ says as he sits down next to me and grins at me over his shoulder.

"You knew I'd want this house." I smile at him.

He nods. "I did. I also knew Mariah would because she seriously loves this neighborhood. But I had to give options."

I sigh as I sit up and glance towards the bathroom where Mariah is still getting ready for our first night in our new house. We decided that we're sleeping here tonight. DJ snuck a few things over here from our apartment so we would have a few items of clothing. He knew we wouldn't want to leave once we stepped foot in it.

Home.

"I sort of didn't think you'd be too happy about it. Considering your old house isn't far away."

He shrugs. "Desiree is in jail for the next three to five years. Layne loves this neighborhood. You love it. We're close to those who mean the world to you. Mariah loves it. Matt is like her brother. So is Luca. She loves Beckett like her own nephew. Desiree won't be back here since her parents are helping her sell the house. This is home. It's home for me. You. Layne. Mariah."

I smile and lean into him. "I really love you."

"I really love you, too." He kisses the tip of my nose as Mariah comes out of the bathroom.

Naked.

My eyes nearly bulge out of my head. DJ almost chokes. It's not that we haven't seen each other naked before. We have. What gets us, though, is the sexy and slow, sultry walk she's doing. She sashays her hips as she walks towards us with a smile that can only be described as shy but devilish. Truly intoxicating.

Just like her.

My eyes are riveted to her. Every curve. Every motion. Right down to her freshly waxed pussy that I truly enjoy burying my tongue in. And she loves every second of it. Probably more than she loves DJ's.

"Holy God, baby girl. What are you doing to us?" DJ's voice is an octave lower than usual. His Texas drawl is a lot more prevalent when he's turned on. And he is *definitely* turned on, if the tenting of his boxer briefs have anything to say about it.

Mariah blinks at him then me. "Why are you two wearing clothes? We never wear clothes to bed."

DJ grins. "I just haven't taken them off yet. And Lyric is exhausted. We might need to help her out a bit."

I blush and stare at Mariah with wide eyes. She's looking at me like a predator. One I certainly don't mind being chased by. Before I have a chance to retort DJ's claim of me being exhausted, though, Mariah is pouncing. She knocks me back on the bed and has her tongue down my throat before I even know what's coming.

"Mmm…" I let her dominate the kiss to her heart's desire because dominant Mariah, even though she still doesn't believe she has a dominant bone in her body, is a very sexy Mariah. One that instantaneously sends heat directly to my core.

Mariah's tongue tangles with mine. She's all over me. Everywhere all at once. Her tongue darts in and out of my mouth. She sucks on my tongue and nips my lower lip, pulling it between her teeth, before she's fucking my mouth again. I don't even realize what she's done until I try to wrap my arms around her, but she's pinned my hands above my head. My pussy pulses. My clit throbs. I arch into her, silently begging her to let me come, and she hasn't even touched me yet.

It's then, with Mariah pinning me to the bed, that I feel DJ. Somehow, he's made his way between my legs and is tugging off my panties.

Only, I don't feel his hands on my hips.

His hands are on my thighs. His teeth are on the waistband of my panties. I gasp when he starts tugging at them. I expect him to pull them down, but he doesn't. He tears the thin fabric until my panties are hanging off one leg.

"DJ!" I squeak.

He rumbles as he kisses and licks his way over my pussy. He teases my clit with his tongue and growls when he thrusts his tongue inside my quivering, wet pussy. "Fuck me, baby. So fucking wet for us already."

"Ah!" I scream into Mariah's mouth when he nips me.

"Mmm…," Mariah moans into my mouth before pressing her tits against mine and starting her domination of my mouth all over again. My body naturally submits to her completely. I buck into her as my thighs tremble. My pussy pulses hard and uncontrollably.

DJ licks my pussy once more before moving onto the other side of my panties. The side still intact. I know it won't be for long, though. I try to close my legs, like it's some kind of instinctual thing or something, but DJ doesn't allow it. He firmly holds them wide apart as his teeth meet the doomed fabric of my panties once more.

Again, he tugs with a low rumble. Mariah, out of control with lust, moans once more into my mouth at the same time DJ rips the rest of my panties with his teeth. Mariah catches my scream with her mouth as she kisses me senseless.

I come so hard and so quickly that my body seems to stop functioning. I tense. My head falls back. Mariah's mouth is on my tits so suddenly that I can't breathe.

"Ah! Fuck! Mariah! DJ! Fuck, yes!" The only part of my body moving is my pussy. Wave after wave of pleasure pulses through me. My pussy spasms again and again. My vision seemingly goes completely black as my orgasm rips through me.

After several moments, I fall limp against the bed, panting heavily.

But I should have known that DJ and Mariah weren't finished with me. They both love watching me come so much that they've made a point of doing it as often as they can. Since we've been together, we find ourselves craving each other, and because of that, we've all found out that we can handle a lot.

Gripping Mariah's hips, I flip her over me. She lets out a surprised squeak, but I can't hold back. I need her. I want her. I crave her taste. I shift to my knees, but just before I can dive into her sweetness, DJ grips my hips.

"Still dripping," he growls. He tugs me to the edge of the bed and pushes my legs apart so my ass is in the air, but I'm level with the steel shaft nudging at my entrance.

I look over my shoulder at him seductively with a shy blush when he leans over me. He kisses me hard as he reaches over me and grips Mariah's thighs. He tugs her down the bed so she's in the perfect position for my mouth to do what it wants to her.

Ravish her.

"Much better," he rumbles against my neck as he kisses it. His dick twitches against me, making me let out a soft whimper as I push back against him. "Take your girl. Let me see how much you want her."

Mariah lets out a quiet sigh of anticipation as she watches and reaches for me. I waste no time. The command from him and her silent one are all I need. I drag my tongue slowly from Mariah's already wet pussy to her clit. I repeat the motion slowly, again and again, savoring one of my two favorite tastes. Once I feel Mariah trembling with the sexiest little moans, I pounce, burying my tongue in her sweet pussy with a moan.

DJ grips my hips and slams into me. Hard. Deep.

"Ah!" I scream into Mariah's pussy. "Fuck, DJ!"

"Lyric!" Mariah screams as she grips the comforter and arches off the bed right into my waiting mouth. My tongue slides deeper into her. Her pussy clamps down around my tongue, making me close my eyes and moan as I push back into DJ.

"Fuck, Lyric," DJ moans as he thrusts. Fast. Hard. So, so deep.

My pussy stretches around him, like he was made for me. I still feel every single ridge of his cock. The largest and thickest cock I've ever seen or had inside me. Who thought nine inches would feel so fucking good? He makes my eyes roll back in my head with every thrust.

The sensations I feel right now overpower everything else in the entire world. I forget my name. I forget how to breathe. I can't think of anything beyond my tongue in Mariah's wet, tight pussy; DJ's delicious thick dick pounding into me.

I moan into Mariah; writhe against DJ. I slam back into him each time he thrusts. He slides deeper as he pulls me into him. My pussy doesn't just hum. It feels like it's full on vibrating. Like if he stops, I'll scream. Beg him to bury himself in me again.

I shake my head against Mariah's pussy. She bucks into me, panting and moaning as she rides my tongue. Her pussy clenches and pulses as uncontrollably as mine is. DJ slams into me, pushing my tongue further into Mariah.

"Fuck, Lyric!" Mariah moans as she tugs my hair and pulls my face even closer to her delectable center.

DJ slaps my ass, making me moan into Mariah's pussy again and clench around him. I feel like my pussy is going to collapse around him, but he keeps thrusting, pushing me higher and higher up Pleasure Mountain. I'm not just going to come for him. I'm going to fucking explode.

"Get her off, baby," DJ rumbles. "I know you love watching her come for you."

He's not wrong. I love watching them both come. So, as DJ rolls his hips against mine and thrusts into me so hard, deep, and fast that I know I'll feel him for days, I set to work on making my girl come all over my tongue. I set my thumb against her clit and tongue fuck her as fast as DJ is pounding into me.

"Yes! Yes! Lyric!"

I feel the exact moment that Mariah loses control. And it sends me right to the brink of my own edge. She comes before I can even say anything. She soaks my tongue, something we don't get her to do often. And as she spasms underneath me and bucks up into me, I feel like my world is about to hit the supernova combustion stage.

I grip Mariah's hips hard as I do my best to lick her clean and help her come down, but DJ's dick feels so good that he has me trembling for him. My pussy pulses so erratically, I'm not sure it's ever going to stop. He keeps pulling me into each hard thrust as he lets out grunts of pleasure. My pussy makes the filthiest, wettest sounds. Sounds that make me blush even as I silently beg him to never stop.

"DJ!" My pussy clamps down hard, but he doesn't stop. He keeps thrusting hard and doing something so amazing as he hits that sweet spot inside me that I know I won't be able to hold on much longer. "DJ, ah! I'm gonna come! Please! Please, let me come!"

He slaps my ass again and grips it. "Come, baby. Let go for me," he commands.

I throw my head back and come hard, screaming. "DJ! Fuck yes! Oh fuck! Yes!" My fingers dig into Mariah's hips as I soak his huge cock.

DJ buries himself in me and holds me firmly as he lets out a roar of his own. "Lyric! Holy fuck, yes!" He comes so hard, I feel like he's gushing into my stomach like a damn geyser.

I collapse against Mariah's thigh as I moan and take all he has to give me. It's like my pussy feeds on his come and greedily sucks it all out of him. And his dick happily gives it up as I squeeze every last drop out of him.

Long after DJ has pulled out and has me and Mariah both tucked into each of his sides with the blankets settled over us, I feel both of my loves fall into a deep, exhausted, and fully satisfied sleep. Then, and only then, do I allow myself to chase them to dreamland, a place I used to hate going because of all the fucked up things that would go on there. Nightmares. Terrors. Horrors.

Now, just like reality, all I find is peace with the loves of my life. My writer and my Texan.

Serenity.

A love I never knew existed.

Home.

Forever and always.

The End

Bonus Chapter!

Chapter Eight

☆ DJ ☆

(At Matt's House the Day of the Celebration of DJ's Divorce)

"We need to talk," Luca growls when Matt and I reach him.

"Given I just had one of the most stressful yet successful and happy days of my life, I hope this talk isn't meant to ruin my mood," I say with narrowed eyes. "I really don't need a lecture."

"Oh, you're getting a lecture alright." Luca's eyes narrow dangerously.

"Play nice," Matt says with a grin.

I follow Luca and Matt to their den after glancing over my shoulder at Mariah. She's busied herself in the kitchen where there are baked goods that smell fucking divine all laid out on the counter. It has to be the work of Lyric because no way in hell Matt or Luca can bake worth a shit.

I glance outside at the people milling around, talking and laughing. I smile because Matt and Luca both know me well. I don't mind the celebration, but I don't want the whole damn department here either. They've only invited a few people who are close to us all. Only the people we invite over here for games when we watch them. It's a good thing we're all off at the same time. And an even better thing is that not all of us are cops. Sometimes it's good to have people on the outside who can keep us from getting too deep into our own blue world.

I close the door to the den behind us and cross my arms over my chest. "So? Let's get it all out in the open."

Matt sits down on the arm of the couch with a grin that Luca might end up smacking off his face. I, however, find it hilarious. I crack a smile, even though I'm attempting to remain serious, and shake my head at him.

"You have a girlfriend. Why my sister?" Luca asks. He tries to look intimidating, and I might believe he is, but even his glare is kind of adorable. Just like his sister.

I raise an eyebrow and bite my lip. "Uh… Well, I'm sure you're aware that all relationships are different. Some happen to have multiple loves."

Luca scoffs. "Don't you dare fucking tell me you're like that dude from that *Sister Wives* show. I don't believe for a second that's real or that he's in love with any of them. He just likes being able to fuck around." He shoots me a glare. "I'm not allowing that to be my sister."

I can't help it. I laugh. "Fuck, Luca. How long have you actually known me? Do you think for a second that I'm anything like that? You know how fucked up my marriage was. You know I never strayed from it, even though I fucking should have."

"Then why my sister?" He yells, but not loud enough to really attract anyone's attention who might be in the house.

Like my girls.

I shoot him a warning glare of my own, but catch Matt's eye. He hasn't moved from the couch, but he's watching us both carefully. I give him a glare, too, just because I can, but then scrub my hands down my face. I'd be the same damn way as Luca is right now if the roles were reversed.

"Okay," I say as I look at him. "Why your sister? Because of the connection. You and Matt have both been talking that girl up to me for years, but mostly over this past year. And just based on a lot of the stuff you told me about her, I started falling for her. Did I want to admit it? No. Nope. No way. Because that would be getting myself into another relationship that I was sure was just going to end in disaster. Just like all of the ones before."

"She doesn't need that shit," Luca says. "She's been through enough."

"But," I continue as if he said nothing. He shuts his mouth. "I realized over the past few months that those previous relationships ended as they did because they were all fucking forced. I never had a connection with any of them. Not like I do with Mariah. Not like I do with Lyric."

"How can you possibly sit there and tell me that you have a connection with her? You've never seen her before today!"

"That's not exactly true, Luca," Matt interjects. "I told you about the day Lyric took down a suspect for us. She may not think I noticed, but I saw the way she looked at DJ. And I saw the way he looked at her. You know all about that."

Luca sighs. "Okay. Fine. One time. You saw her one time before today. That's lust. Not a connection. I know how pretty she is."

Matt chuckles before I can say anything. "Are you saying you can't fall in love at first sight?"

Luca turns to Matt and throws his hands up. "Yes!" He looks back at me. "See? He gets it."

"Well -" I start.

"Luca," Matt says, interrupting me once more. "You don't believe that anymore than any of us in this room does. Because if you did, then you'd feel like you and I fell into lust. Not love."

Luca's eyes snap to Matt's before they narrow. I bite my lip and lean back against the wall. Luca sighs as he relents. "Okay, fine." He turns back to me as he slumps into Matt's lap. Matt wraps his arms around his waist and kisses his neck.

"I had a connection with her, Luca," I start. "And it's not just that I think she's hot. She is. I'm not going to sit here and lie to you. Lyric is gorgeous. But it's not just her looks. It's everything you've told me about her. It's…" I close my eyes and let out a breath before opening them. "It's her reaction to me and Mariah. It's the way she looks in my shirt. How my scent calms her. It's her creativity. Her strength. It's the fire I see simmering underneath just waiting to be let out. But most of all, Luca, it's her. It's all of her. The entire package. Reactions and connections are all just a part of it. She's special. One of a kind. She's the piece of both me and Mariah that we feel like we're missing. The piece that we both feel like she fills. Is it fucked up to love two people?" I shrug as I push off the wall. "Hell, I don't know. But I also don't care. You know better than anyone that nothing is going to stand in the way of true love." I glance at Matt who's smirking behind Luca's head, even though he's trying to hide it in his neck.

Luca is quiet for a long while before he stands and paces. Matt and I both watch as a torrent of emotions plays over his features. Finally, he takes a deep breath and looks at me. He opens his mouth a few times before any words actually come out. What he says, though, I would have never expected.

"Lyric was beaten by her ex."

I just blink at him. My heart stops cold in my chest. I see red and mentally shake myself out of the murderous black hole I just about fell into you. "What?" I ask hoarsely after a few moments.

Luca seemingly collapses back onto Matt's lap. Matt wraps around him once more. Luca runs his hand through his hair and lets out a breath. "Yeah."

I lean back against the wall again and slide down it until I'm sitting on the floor. "Just… what…?" I shake my head, unable to wrap my mind around what he just told me.

"Yeah," Luca says again as he clears his throat. "Lyric has always been… different. Submissive, yes. Shy and quiet. Yes. But there has always been something else about her. Something… I don't know. Something that men found irresistible and women found intimidating. She was never a leader. Always a follower. But she was also never a doormat. I think that… confidence?" He pauses as if thinking about the word. Finally, he nods. "Confidence. That confidence was something men flocked to. But women found it off-putting. We grew up in a family where women had a certain role. Take care of the family. Lyric shocked everyone and decided to go to college for Beauty Therapy. And she passed with flying colors. To the outside world, she was rebellious. But those of us who knew her, well, we knew the real her."

I rub my eyes and pinch the bridge of my nose. "I hate that I already know where this is going."

Luca huffs. "Her first boyfriend, to all of us, was a good guy. He always portrayed the utmost respect and support of her and her goals. But behind closed doors, he was beating her down. Literally and figuratively. Everyone wondered why we suddenly stopped seeing her. Especially me. We've always been close. She always had a new excuse about why she couldn't go to coffee with me. Or just anywhere at all. One day, I showed up at her apartment. She had bruises all over. Turns out, her perfect boyfriend wasn't so perfect. I took her to my place. She was never the same after that."

Matt takes a breath as he takes over for an emotionally distraught Luca. "She was with him for a long time. No one knew that he'd do shit to her to force her to bend to his will. He always told her he was breaking her rebellious side and making her into the perfect woman. Apparently, the perfect woman to him was someone who did everything he said, when he said it, with no questions asked. And by everything, I mean everything. If she was sick and he wanted sex? She best not say no."

"Christ." I rub my temples.

"Needless to say," Luca continues after taking a little time to compose himself. He takes a deep breath and stands and paces again. "She thinks sex is all she's good for. She had two relationships after him. Neither of them hurt her. At least physically. Mentally? Well, she was already low. So, once they'd gotten enough sex out of her, they broke it off. She was left wondering what she'd done wrong. By the time it was all over, that confidence that women were intimidated by was gone. She was just another girl they could bully and use to make themselves feel better. Our snobby bitch of a sister and her friends included."

"I'm so pissed off for her, I'm vibrating. Fuck, I don't..." I shake my head and lean it back against the wall. "I don't even know what to say."

"My point, DJ, is I'm scared for her. I know who you are as a man. And hell, I know damn well you'd be good for her. But she's my sister. And she's been through so much in her life. I don't want to see her in a relationship where she's second best. Because she's not. She needs to be treated like the amazing woman she is. Matt and I have spent years working with her to make her see that. I don't want her to feel like she isn't as important to you or Mariah as the both of you are to each other."

I nod as I stand. "I get it, Luca. I do. But I'm not like that. My feelings are genuine for both Lyric and Mariah. I'm not going to fuck this up. Those two are far too important. I've never felt like this before. And I know Mariah hasn't either. About me or Lyric."

Luca watches me for a few moments. I hold his gaze to prove to him I'm in this for the long haul. Finally, Luca nods. "She'll try to fade in the background to make sure you and Mariah are happy."

I shake my head. "We won't let her. I won't. She's a part of this. A part of us. She's an equal partner."

Luca crosses his arms over his touch. "Touch. Actions. It's how she expresses herself. She thinks she sucks at explaining her feelings and expressing them with words. So she does it through actions. She'll reach for you for comfort but pull away because she's unsure and doesn't want to come off clingy."

"She can touch me all she wants."

"She'll reach for your waistband. Not your shirt. Not your pant leg. Your waistband. I don't know why, but that's where she finds the most comfort and connection."

I raise an eyebrow. "Are you trying to warn me, or make me run away? Because I'm not going anywhere. If she needs to be held, I'll do it. With no hesitation. I'm not going to push her away if she hugs me. And I sure as hell won't shove her off me if she tries to touch me. I'll give her all she needs. And because I know you need to hear this, so will Mariah. We'll all give her and each other what we need because that's how relationships work."

"She has a demon. Just like Rih," Matt says raspily. "Hers is a female. Vicious as fuck."

I shrug. "You know damn well I can deal with Mariah's. No way in fuck I won't be able to deal with Lyric's."

"She chews straws or the inside of her cheek when she's anxious. Sometimes, she bites her lip. You'll need to watch for that because last time she didn't even notice she had blood dripping from it," Luca tells me.

"Mariah does the same thing. Really, Luca. I got her. I won't fuck up."

"Sometimes, she stays up all night. She'll try to hide it, but you can tell," Matt says. "She'll zone out on you in the middle of conversations. Once, she walked outside in a rainstorm in just a hoodie.

Nothing else. My neighbor called me because he saw her from his upstairs window. No fucking clue how long she'd been out there, but she was soaked and he could see all she had to offer. When I got back here, she was peaceful as fuck, but sick for two weeks. To this day, she tries to run outside in storms."

I smile a little. "Mariah loves the rain. It quiets her mind, too. But if it's something I need to watch for, I'll make sure and watch for it. Even if that means hourly check-ins. I'll figure it out." I look at Luca. "I'll figure it out, man. You know me well. You know I won't hurt her and do all I can to protect her and show her love. I'll help her see her worth. I'll do whatever it takes."

Luca lets out a breath and nods as he closes his eyes. I can almost see the weight lifting off his shoulders when his eyes open. "Fuck, I know. I know DJ. I guess I just... I need the reassurance that she's going to be okay."

"If she gets hurt, I'll help you dig my grave and willingly jump into it. How's that?" I give him a teasing grin, but I know he knows how serious I am. I don't ever want to be the one to hurt either of my girls.

Luca chuckles and holds out a hand for me to shake. I take it, but he pulls me into a hug instead. After a few moments, he lets me go. No more words are said. None are needed. Luca told me all he needed to and a lot that he didn't. I didn't expect to be told about Lyric's past. At least not from him. I believed Lyric would tell me in her own time. I still believe she'll tell me what he didn't when she's ready.

So, with Luca's words heavy on my shoulders, I follow him and Matt back out into the main part of the house. My eyes immediately find Mariah's, and I grin when I see Lyric next to her. She's still wearing my shirt. The one I left here after our last game night. I came here right after I'd gotten done with serving an unexpected weekend warrant with SWAT. I borrowed one of Matt's shirts because that one was soaked in sweat. He mentioned he washed it, but we both kept forgetting about it each time I was here. But I was close enough to Lyric to still smell the faint scent of my cologne.

I've never been so glad about forgetting one of my favorite shirts here because it looks a lot better on her than it does me.

This is what it's all about. The little moments. Moments like this that I'll never forget. How shy they both look. How they light up when they see me.

As I make my way across the room, I can't help but think how the words I spoke to Luca are more than one-hundred percent accurate. These two girls are my life now.

And that isn't something I'd ever fuck up.

Concluding The Beautiful Dream Series

The sweet and sinfully sexy Beautiful Dream Series concludes with
Unveiling Our Passions.

Runaway.

That's what I'm called back home. A runaway. No one seems to believe
that I didn't actually run. I left because it was the only way for me to
survive. That if I hadn't, I would've given into the demon that torments me
daily.

Two years later, in the Florida sun, I'm finally free of the suppression that
held me down.

But not from the darkness.

I exist in a world that frightens me and keeps me moving in one direction. I
walk a very straight line down the path of safety. Assurance. Where no one
can hurt me except the evil fiend in my mind.

Until one day, my entire world is flipped on its head. I'm shoved violently
into the midnight blackness that exists in my own head.

Then, a glint of light comes in the form of two men. Two police officers
with the Gainesville Police Department. They want to be my light in the
darkness. To help me destroy it.

They're determined to prove that love is the greatest weapon of all.

While I want to believe them, I'm not sure I can. Sometimes, the pull of
the shadow world is too strong…

Order ***Unveiling Our Passions*** Today!

The Beautiful Dream Series

Available Now

Loving You
My Love, My Heart
Softening Lyric
Undercover Temptations
Captain Charming
Breaking Boundaries
Crashing Into You
Tactical Inferno
Ravishing Our Queen
Cherished By The Texan
Unveiling Our Passions

Box Sets Available

The Beautiful Dream Series: Box Set: Part 1
The Beautiful Dream Series: Box Set: Part 2

Other Books By Melony Ann
The Crane Family Series

Available Now

The Reluctant Mafia King
Sweet Lies
Billion Dollar Love Story
Be Mine
Protecting Her
Dangerously Forbidden Love
His Heart
Love In The Dark

Box Sets Available

The Crane Family Series

The Deimos Trilogy

Available Now

Connor's Legacy
Aryan's Alpha
Kade's Redemption

Box Sets Available

The Deimos Trilogy

The Forbidden Temptation Series

Available Now

The Detective's Forbidden Temptation
The Running Back's Forbidden Temptation

The Lucinio Family Series

Available Now

Rising From The Ashes
The Player's Rebel
Encrypting My Heart

Multi Author Series
Piper Falls: Firehouse 49

Available Now

Ignite My Fire by Melony Ann
Regain My Fire by Kindra White
Playing With My Fire by D.L. Howe
Fight My Fire by Darley Collins
Against My Fire by Anneke Boshoff
Relight My Fire by Louise Murchie
Harness My Fire by Ayana Lisbet
Quench My Fire by Havana Wilder

Let's Be Friends

Follow me on

Bookbub

Facebook

Goodreads

Instagram

Tik Tok

Visit my website
www.melonyannauthor.com

Subscribe to my newsletter and get a FREE never-seen-before NOVELLA
just for subscribers!
https://www.melonyannauthor.com/exclusive-content

Join my Facebook Reader Group!
Melony Ann's Sizzling Book Nook

The official Beautiful Dream Series Playlist on YouTube
https://youtube.com/playlist?list=PLGEiD5wbQmDe1z4_FeeKbMLcBkOz
1M4L4

Dedication

When we feel like we're drowning and can't find our way to the surface, your light guides us; pulls us from the viciousness of our demon's grasp.

Acknowledgements

Brad - I never knew the true meaning of the words "everything I do, I do it for you." Not until you. You've sacrificed so much of your life for other people and taught me the true meaning of selflessness. I love you so much it hurts to breathe sometimes. I'll never give you up. And I'll never be strong enough to let you go. Thankfully, I don't ever have to.

Laura - You're the sunshine in a very dark world. The light I crave but could never quite grasp. I love you beyond words and am so honored that you chose me. Well. Us. But mostly me. Because, you know. It's all me. Kidding, of course. The truth, though, is that I love you so much and refuse to allow you to be anywhere but right here where you belong.

Jay - I truly hate when things are delayed. Like, you know, flights. But I will forever be grateful to Delta for being delayed way back on that fateful day in 2009. Because if those pilots hadn't had to go back to Minneapolis the night before, we never would have met. And wouldn't have gotten to experience the kind of love only found once in a lifetime. Our love. I know you hear it all the time from us, but I really do love you and am so grateful to call you mine.

Anneke - When beautiful souls cross my path, I tend to covet them and put them on my fictional shelf so they never get lost. Yours is front and center. I'm so honored to have you in my life and beyond grateful that you've supported me and inspired me to keep going for so long. Love you!

Jason - They say lightning doesn't strike twice. Well, I think they lie because if they were telling the truth, I wouldn't have you.

Kayla - Right along with Anneke, you're the pride of my soul collection. It sounds a little morbid and dark, but it's the way I look at it. Thank you for being a beautiful soul.

To the Bookstagram Community.

To my family.

To all of those who believe in me and support me.

To all of those who don't.

Cover by: Carter Cover Designs

Edited by: Alyssa Skaggs

About Melony Ann

Melony Ann began writing short stories and poetry as a child. She continued honing her craft over the years until she took the plunge and began publishing her work, despite having severe anxiety.

Melony writes contemporary romance stories that are full of suspense and a lot of steam.

When she isn't writing, she is loving her family and working to make her life something she deserves.

Melony believes that if her writing can inspire just one person, then all of her hard work is worth it.

Her hope is that her writing allows each and every one of her readers to escape for a little while. To dive into a different world one book at a time.